A CAVALCADE OF
DRAGONS

A CAVALCADE OF

DRAGONS

EDITED BY
ROGER LANCELYN GREEN

ILLUSTRATED BY
KRYSTYNA TURSKA

A lake and a fairy boat
To sail in the moonlight clear—
And merrily we would float
From the Dragons that watch us here!
Thomas Hood

NEW YORK · HENRY Z. WALCK, INC.

First published in Great Britain 1970
as The Hamish Hamilton Book of Dragons
© 1970 ROGER LANCELYN GREEN
Illustrations © 1970 KRYSTYNA TURSKA
All rights reserved
ISBN: 8098-2413-2
Library of Congress Catalog Card Number: 72-118776

Printed in Great Britain

Dedicated To

J. R. R. TOLKIEN

We were talking of DRAGONS,   Tolkien and I
In a Berkshire bar.   The big workman
Who had sat silent   and sucked his pipe
All the evening,   from his empty mug
With gleaming eye   glanced towards us:
"I seen 'em myself!"   he said fiercely.

C. S. Lewis

Contents

Introduction

WHAT is a Dragon? Many years ago when I was teaching in a Prep School for a short time during the War, I used to be asked this question when telling such tales as Beowulf or Sigurd or the Argonauts, and I made up a kind of Just So Story in answer.

"In the high and far off times, O Best Beloved", there were no zoos which anyone who liked could visit to see what animals from other lands looked like. And there were no photographs, either—and travellers who had actually seen lions and tigers and crocodiles were not usually very good at drawing. They described what a leopard looked like, for example, and an artist drew three leopards for the Royal Standard; and the painters of inn signs tried to turn these back into natural rather than heraldic animals. But their leopards looked much more like cats, and the leopard's hideous snarl of anger quite easily looked more like a grin—certainly in Cheshire. (Indeed at Brimstage, near my home, there is a medieval carving of a cat's head with a definite grin—probably meant to be a snarling leopard.)

Now, a traveller from the East would come home and tell stories of what he had seen. "I saw a great creature like a wild cat, but a hundred times bigger. It had huge white claws sharp enough to tear one in pieces; and it had big eyes that seemed to flame, and long, sharp teeth. But I heard of a creature with much worse teeth: it lived in a cave by the River Nile, and was like a lizard but at least *two* hundred times bigger. It had huge jaws many feet long, and could lift the top one up so that it could swallow a man whole—but it didn't need to, because it had sharp teeth like a saw on both its top and its bottom jaw. . . . And I met a man who told me about serpents in India who are fifty feet long and can swallow an ox whole: they are covered in scales, but not as hard ones as the crocodile in Egypt. . . . And some snakes can just look at a bird—or, I expect, a man—and charm it so that it cannot run away but walks up to it—just as an adder at home fascinates a bird, or a stoat

ix

catches a rabbit. . . . Oh, and they say some snakes drop poison out of their mouths so venomous that it burns like liquid fire. . . . And some of the birds in those distant lands are said to be big and strong enough to carry off full grown sheep: I've heard it said they can even carry off a cow. . . . Some people say that there are birds with beaks like an eagle and the body of a lion: these are called griffins or gryphons. I've never seen one, but a crusader whom I met had seen huge carved figures of them in Greece."

The people who heard these descriptions of lions, crocodiles, pythons, cobras, eagles and the carved sphinxes and gryphons of the Naxian Treasury at Delphi can have got very little in the way of a clear picture of what all these creatures really looked like. And when they came to re-tell what they had heard, some of them may well have got muddled:

"A man I know who had been on pilgrimage to Jerusalem saw the most amazing creatures in the East. There was one like a lion, but it had wings; and another like a huge snake, but with great jaws armed with teeth that could swallow an ox or bite off a man's leg in a moment. And one of them, but I forget which, had such a poisonous breath that it burnt like fire."

And then one of his hearers (perhaps waking up next morning with a hang-over after too much mead or malmsey) would try to remember what he had been told by the man he met last night who had such fascinating stories about the creatures in the East: "Now what was that monster like? It had claws and paws like a lion, and a mouth full of huge teeth, and a great body all covered with scales and big wings, and a long tail like a serpent. Oh yes, and didn't he say it breathed fire?"

Then he would tell all this to a friend who had been brought up in a monastery, or had been a "clerke of Oxenford" who would exclaim pityingly: "But my dear fellow, that's a Dragon. You can read all about them in Pliny's *Natural History* or Aelian's *Nature of Animals*. And there were saints like St. Philip who killed a Dragon at Hierapolis; and St. George of course. . . . "

And all the time, doubtless, there would be folk tales about Dragons being told in the poorer homes, and lays being sung or romances recited in the halls and castles: about the Lambton Worm or St. George and the Dragon, maybe; about Sir Tristram and the Irish Dragon, or Sir Launcelot's Dragon— to say nothing of the stories of Saints other than George who killed Dragons by more miraculous means.

And finally, if the more learned scholars disbelieved in Dragons, what about the fossilized bones that turned up in caves and were dug up every now and then? Of course they knew nothing in those days about dinosaurs and pterodactyls and the diplodocus. . . . Indeed, Dragons were believed in until about three hundred years ago, and by the time their actual existence ceased to be accepted, they had won their way into poetry—and were soon to return in fiction.

In this Book of Dragons I have tried to collect as many of the earlier stories as possible—from ancient Greece and Rome, Iceland and Denmark of the Sagas, Byzantium, Medieval Romances, folk tales and fairy tales of many lands—to lead on to the literary tales, by way of Spenser, to E. Nesbit, right down to Tolkien and Lewis.

But there are many more later tales of Dragons to read. Not only short stories—and E. Nesbit wrote a whole *Book of Dragons* from which only one is included here—but longer books which would be spoilt by having their Dragons cut out and served separately.

There is Kenneth Grahame's *The Reluctant Dragon*, most famous of the Dragons of Later Days—whose story was too long to include here. But it can be found quite easily in many collections of Modern Fairy Stories, or in its original place in *Dream Days*.

And there is the splendid battle between the Fire Dragon and the Ice Dragon in Andrew Lang's *Prince Prigio*; Tolkien's *Farmer Giles of Ham* which is largely concerned with a Dragon, and his magnificent northern Dragon, Smaug, in *The Hobbit*; even my own Dragon who plays such a large part in *The Wonderful Stranger*. And there is the unexpected Dragon in *The Voyage of the "Dawn Treader"* by C. S. Lewis who simply must be met in his own cave by anyone interested in Dragons. . . .

At least may I hope that, after reading this book, none of you will be like Eustace in Lewis's story—*before* his experiences with the Dragon:

"Edmund or Lucy or you would have recognized it at once, but Eustace had read none of the right books. The thing that came out of the cave was something he had never even imagined—a long lead-coloured snout, dull red eyes, no feathers or fur, a long lithe body that trailed on the ground, legs whose elbows went up higher than its back like a spider's, cruel claws, bats' wings that made a rasping noise on the stones, yards of tail. And the two lines of smoke were coming from its two nostrils. He never said the word *Dragon* to himself . . ."

PART ONE

Dragons of Ancient Days

Jason and the Dragon of Colchis

LONG ago there lived in the beautiful land of Greece a Prince called Jason. To win back his father's kingdom of Iolchos he set out on the quest of the Golden Fleece, sailing over unknown seas in the ship *Argo* with many of the young princes and heroes of Greece as his companions.

After many adventures Jason and the Argonauts came to the red river Phasis that flowed down from the Caucasus to the Black Sea, to the city of Colchis where Aeëtes the Wizard was king.

The Golden Fleece hung on a great tree in a wood surrounded by a high wall behind the palace, and round the tree coiled a huge Dragon that never slept.

King Aeëtes greeted Jason and his companions kindly and entertained them in the palace. But when Jason told him the reason for their coming, Aeëtes smiled darkly and said: "I have always known that one day Greeks would come in quest of the Golden Fleece—for indeed it came from Greece in my father's day. . . . Yes, you may take away the Golden Fleece if the gods will that you should. . . . But to prove whether or not you are appointed to do so, you must harness my bulls to the plough, sow the seed I shall give to you, and reap the crop which will grow immediately from the ground. Tomorrow you shall do this: tonight we feast."

When he heard this, Jason was greatly troubled. For the two brazen-footed bulls of King Aeetes breathed fire, and Jason had heard that the seed which he had to sow was dragons' teeth—which brought forth a crop of armed men.

But the gods of Greece were on his side, and in particular Aphrodite, the goddess of love. She cast her magic over Medea, the daughter of King Aeetes, so that the dark witch-maiden fell so deeply in love with Jason that nothing else in the world mattered to her but to win him for her husband.

So, when the feast was over, Medea came silently through the night to where Jason sat with his head in his hands thinking and plotting how to overcome the bulls— or how to steal away the Golden Fleece and flee from Colchis before the morning light.

He looked up and saw the beautiful, dark-haired, dark-eyed princess of Colchis standing gazing down at him. And the love in her eyes kindled desire in him so that he rose slowly, without a word and held out his arms to her.

In a little while she put him from her and said:

"Prince Jason, for the love I bear you I will help you to harness the brazen-footed bulls and sow the furrow of death with dragons' teeth, and reap the crop that will rise from the earth. For love of you I will show you how to steal away the Golden Fleece from the Grove of Hecate and escape with it from my father, who plots your death. But before I do this, and betray my father and my country, swear to me by the most sacred oath known to the men of Greece that you will take me with you in your flight, and make me your wife and set me by your side on the throne of Iolchos when at length the *Argo* comes home again to the rocky slopes of Pelion."

Then Jason swore to marry her, binding himself by the oath on the Styx, the River of the Dead, which binds even the gods themselves.

After this, Medea went to the temple of Hecate, goddess of Witches, of which she was chief priestess, and there brewed a magic ointment. This was made from the juice of a red flower that grew high on the slopes of Caucasus and sprang from the blood of Prometheus, the Titan who lay chained to the summit of the mountain. Now Prometheus was immortal, and came of the race of the gods, so that in his veins flowed the divine ichor—the blood of the gods—which does not dry up and turn black as blood does but lives and shines red and fresh for ever.

In the first flush of dawn Medea came again to Jason, roused him from sleep and gave him the magic ointment, whispering certain words of advice to him as well about all that lay before him.

When full day was come the messengers of King Aeetes arrived to bring the Argonauts to the field where Jason must sow the dragons' teeth. And Jason came gladly, having anointed his body all over with the magic ointment, and remembering all that Medea had told him.

When the brazen-footed bulls were released from their stable they charged at Jason, breathing fire out of their nostrils.

Then all looked to see Jason burnt into ashes by the fire: but the flames turned aside from the immortal blood of Prometheus, and Jason seized the bulls, harnessed them to the plough, and was soon urging them up and down the furrows as the moist soil turned in long ribbons of turf beneath the share of bronze.

Aeetes scowled with fury, but the Argonauts cheered as Jason finished his ploughing and asked for the seed to sow.

Without a word the king handed him a great golden helmet that rattled as he shook it in his anger. Jason took the helmet and setting it in the crook of his left arm like a corn-measure went down the furrows scattering the dragons' teeth on either side as a farmer sows grain.

As he drew towards the end of the field he heard the clash of arms behind him and cries of warning from the Argonauts. As soon as he had thrown the last handful of dragons' teeth he spun round on his heel—and saw that all over the field behind him armed men were rising out of the ground and advancing threateningly towards him.

Raising the golden helmet above his head, Jason flung it into the midst of the earth-men. At once they turned upon each other, hewing and smiting with their swords until all lay dead.

"And now, King of Colchis," cried Jason striding up to Aeetes, "fulfil your promise! Give me the Golden Fleece and let me sail away in peace!"

"I will give it you tomorrow!" hissed Aeetes, his eyes full of fear and hatred; and he turned and strode into the palace.

When darkness fell Medea came again to Jason.

"My father plans to seize the *Argo* early in the morning and burn it and all of you to ashes," she said. "Therefore we must go tonight. Bid your men be ready on board to sail at a moment's notice, and come with me to the Grove of Hecate to take the Golden Fleece. We have still the Dragon who guards it to overcome—but maybe your strength and my magic may prevail against him."

Jason gave his orders to the Argonauts, who stole quietly away to the harbour where the *Argo* lay, and then turned to follow Medea. But Orpheus, one of the Argonauts had lingered behind, and now he said:

"Let me come also, for I have the power of magic in my songs and in the music of my lyre."

So Medea led the way by secret paths and doors of which she, as priestess of Hecate, had the key, until they came out into a grove of mighty trees with trunks towering up like the pillars of a greater temple than man could build.

Here they were met by Melanion, Guardian of the Grove, leading a kid for the Dragon's evening meal. Jason had already spoken with Melanion, who was anxious to join the Argonauts and escape with them to Greece—so he welcomed him with a nod.

Through the great, dark Grove they stole like shadows, in and out of the long streaks and pools of moonlight, until they drew towards the grey ilex tree on which hung the Golden Fleece.

As they came nearer, the white light of the moon seemed to fade into the gold light of morning, and they realized that it was the Fleece itself shining on the tree above them.

Jason moved eagerly towards it, and then stopped suddenly with a gasp, and drew back. For round the tree coiled the great Dragon, its green and blue scales glimmering in the strange light, but its eyes burning red and angry as it opened its mouth and let out a strange cry that was half a hiss and half a roar.

Now Melanion stepped forward and released the kid. For a moment the creature stood shaking with fear; then the Dragon's eyes caught and held it—held it and drew it until with a little, pathetic bleat the kid leapt into its very jaws.

In a moment it was gone. But the Dragon did not lie its head down as usual, for it scented the strangers. It began waving it slowly from side to side, its eyes flashing, as

if trying to catch one of them as it had caught the kid.

"Play and sing!" whispered Medea. And Orpheus turned aside, struck the strings of his lyre, and began to sing the Hymn to Sleep which he had written. As he sang the Grove grew stiller and stiller: Jason, Melanion and Medea felt their eyelids growing heavy and had to use all their will-power to keep awake.

But the Dragon slowly lowered its head. The flame died out of its eyes, and presently they closed.

Swiftly Medea sprang forward, sprinkled some drops of a magic brew over its head, and then returned to Jason.

"It will not wake easily now," she said. "But do not try to harm it. If your sword did not kill it at the first blow, then it would wake indeed—and we would not live for long."

So Jason stole forward, set his feet on the scaly coils of the very Dragon itself, and climbed up to the ilex tree. Seizing the Golden Fleece, he tore it from its nails, sped down his living ladder, and away through the Grove, led by Medea and followed by his two companions, to seek safety on the *Argo*.

The Song that Orpheus Sang to Charm the Dragon

Translated by ANDREW LANG

Sleep! King of Gods and men!
Come to my call again,
Swift over field and fen,
   Mountain and deep:
Come, bid the waves be still;
Sleep, streams on height and hill;
Beasts, birds, and snakes, thy will
   Conquereth, Sleep!
Come on thy golden wings,
Come ere the swallow sings,
Lulling all living things,
   Fly they or creep!
Come with thy leaden wand,
Come with thy kindly hand,
Soothing on sea or land
   Mortals that weep.
Come from the cloudy west,
Soft over brain and breast,
Bidding the Dragon rest,
   Come to me, Sleep!

The Boy and the Dragon

IN the days when Arcadia was the wildest and loneliest part of Greece there lived a boy called Thoas whose home was in a village of only two or three houses where the shepherds dwelt who fed their flocks on the lower slopes of the mountains.

Thoas loved to wander alone among the rocks and caves higher up the mountains. Unlike his brothers and their friends he did not care for hunting and killing the wild creatures of Arcadia, but would make friends with them— sitting still for hours at a time until the very bear cubs would come and rub their heads against him.

One day, clambering higher than ever before, he came to a lofty ledge of rock at the foot of a still higher cliff, and paused in surprise. For there, all by itself, was a baby dragon not two feet long.

Thoas knew that there were dragons far up on the mountains, higher than he had ever been able to climb: he had seen them occasionally, so far away that they might have been no more than eagles. But he had never come closer to one, and he now looked with great interest and excitement at the little dragon on the ledge.

Very soon he saw that it was weak as if from want or food and water, and realized that it must have fallen or fluttered down the cliff from somewhere far above.

Gently Thoas took up the little dragon in his arms and

carried it down the mountain side until he came to a
stream. Here he let it drink, and fed it with fruit and herbs,
until it seemed to be recovering from its weakness.

He expected that it would run away in search of its
mother; but instead, when he got up to go home, the
dragon followed him. Whenever he paused it rubbed its
head against his legs, making a hissing noise that might
almost have been a purr.

Thoas brought the dragon all the way to his village and
settled it on his own bed in the little cave in the rock
against which his father's house of rough stones and wood
was built.

The shepherd and his elder sons wished to kill the dragon
immediately. But Thoas begged them to spare it:

"He would have died if I had left him on the ledge," he
said. "And when I had carried him down and fed him, he
followed me of his own free will. I will keep him in my
cave, and feed him. He does no harm, and eats only fruit
and herbs."

"It will be different when he grows to full size," said the
shepherd. "Then he will be taking our lambs, and later the
sheep themselves."

But he was not an unkind man, and he at length allowed
Thoas to keep his strange pet "for a time at least".

So Thoas kept the little dragon in his cave and fed and tended it. During the day, wherever Thoas went, the dragon followed him; and at night they slept in the same bed—for this sort of dragon did not breathe fire.

The dragon grew very quickly, however, and Thoas found it more and more difficult to collect enough fruit and herbs to satisfy it. But still each evening they would share Thoas's bowl of wine, and then sleep soundly on the bed in the cave.

The shepherd, however, was troubled. "That dragon will very soon become dangerous," he said to the other shepherds as they sat under the big oak tree in the village sipping their strong drink distilled out of the skins and pips left over after making the wine.

Then each would tell terrible tales of dragons who had come down from the mountains and devoured whole flocks of sheep, and sometimes eaten the shepherd himself so that not a trace was left.

Soon they decided that they must get rid of the dragon. The shepherd knew that Thoas would be heartbroken if they simply killed it, so he devised a scheme to which his friends agreed reluctantly.

One evening they mixed strong spirits with the wine that Thoas and the dragon had before going to bed, so that the two sank into such a deep sleep that nothing would wake them.

Then the shepherd and his friends took up the bed with Thoas and the dragon on it, and carried it away to a distant, stony hillside. Here they left the dragon, and brought Thoas back to his cave, still sleeping.

Next morning Thoas looked in vain for his dragon, and was very sad and troubled at his loss.

"The time had come for him to seek his own kind," said the shepherd. "No wild creature will stay with us for long. Do not grieve, it is best so. But think of him with a mate and baby dragons of his own, happy in a cave near the mountain tops where no man could ever climb."

So Thoas did not seek for the dragon, and in time got over his regret for the loss of his strange companion, and made friends with other and more usual creatures.

But a few years later when he was already almost a grown man, Thoas happened to be on a journey through the mountains with a store of wool to sell at one of the small towns on the coast of Arcadia.

In a lonely pass he was set upon by a band of robbers who not only took the wool, but began to beat him cruelly.

Partly with the pain, and partly in case any assistance might be near, Thoas cried out for help as loudly as he could.

Dragons can see further and hear more acutely than any other creatures; and now, in his cave far up on the mountain high above, the dragon heard and recognized the voice of his long-ago friend.

Down he came like a storm cloud, hissing and roaring so terribly that the robbers turned and fled in terror—only to fall one by one beneath the claws of the dragon.

When all were dead, the dragon returned to where Thoas was lying insensible. Very carefully he lifted him and bore him away to his cave in the mountains. There Thoas lived for many days, the great dragon bringing him food and pouring water on his wounds until he was quite recovered from the cruel attack of the robbers.

Then the dragon took Thoas up once more in his mighty claws and carried him over hill and valley to the very hillside where he himself had been left by the shepherds.

There he left him, and Thoas walked back in safety to his village where he told the strange tale of the dragon who had remembered an old friend and come to save him from mortal danger, bearing no grudge for having himself been cast out and left in the wilderness.

The Dragon of Macedon

IN ancient times the country to the north of Greece was called Emathia. But when King Macedon ruled over it, bringing peace and prosperity, the people changed its name in honour of their greatest king—nor did any greater rule over it for many hundreds of years until Alexander the Great inherited the kingdom and set out to conquer the world.

King Macedon had many sons, the eldest of whom was Pindus, the tallest and most handsome man of his day. When King Macedon died, Pindus succeeded to the throne, and seemed likely to be as good a king as his father, and as much beloved by his people.

But his brothers were jealous of him, and they conspired together, and at length drove him from the throne.

Pindus might have made war against his brothers, for most of the Macedonians were faithful to him. But he did not wish to bring about civil war, or to harm his brothers, in spite of their wickedness, and he made no attempt to win back the throne. Instead, he devoted all his time to hunting, and soon became famous throughout all Greece for his skill at the chase.

One day he was pursuing some young wild mules, and spurring his horse after them, left far behind those who were hunting with him. The mules sought shelter in a deep cavern and disappeared from sight, so Pindus leapt from his horse, tied it to the nearest tree, and prepared to follow them into the cave.

As he was about to enter, a voice cried: "Do not touch the mules!"

Who called he could not see, for the rocks caught the words and echoed them from all sides.

Being unable to discover who had called to him so mysteriously, and feeling that it might be some god warning him for his good, Pindus turned back, mounted his horse, and left the place.

Next day as he hunted alone he drew near to the same place, and paused in doubt near the cavern. He did not dare to enter it, but began looking about to see if any mountain shepherds or hunters lived near the spot who might have warned him on the previous day.

Suddenly, while he searched, there came out of the cavern into which the mules had disappeared a dragon of immense size, its great neck and head arching up above his own, and its tongue flicking hungrily from side to side between its sharp white fangs.

Though desperately afraid, Pindus did not turn to fly. For he thought: "The dragon can move much faster than I, and will simply sink its teeth into my back and drag me off to its cave. There is no escape, but I'd rather die facing my foe than fleeing from him."

The dragon did not seem to be in an angry mood, and made no attempt to attack Pindus, but stood over him swaying its head from side to side and hissing softly.

A desperate thought came to Pindus. At his belt hung some partridges and a young deer which he had caught that morning. Kneeling down, he offered these to the dragon, saying: "Take all I have. Spare me, and I will bring you each day half of what I take in the chase."

It is to be doubted whether the dragon understood the words, but it seemed to understand the action. For it seized the birds and the deer in its jaws, and turning, carried them off into the cave, where it disappeared from sight.

Pindus backed slowly away to where he had tied his horse, leapt upon its back, and galloped thankfully down the valley to safety.

But it seemed to him that he had made a promise which he must keep. So each evening he would carry half the spoils of the chase and lay them outside the dragon's cave.

He did not see the great creature again, but the offerings vanished each night, and it seemed also that extra good fortune attended him in his hunting from that day on. Not only did he catch far more than ever before, but as he himself grew both more handsome and more famous as a hunter, more and more followed him in the chase, both men and women.

All this made his brothers even more jealous than when he was king, and they began to plot how they might murder him.

Their chance came one day when he had gone out hunting alone, and they were able to lay an ambush for him, attack him suddenly from all sides, and soon dispatch him.

As he died, however, Pindus cried out once for help, and his voice went ringing away into the mountains and ended in one long despairing cry that echoed from rock to rock and whispered away into silence.

The dragon in the great cave heard that cry, recognized the voice of the man whose life he had once spared, and who had ever afterwards fed him so faithfully, and came at full speed to see what was happening.

When he saw Pindus lying dead, bleeding from many wounds, and the wicked brothers standing round with

their tell-tale swords still bloody in their hands, he swooped down upon them, screaming with rage.

The brothers turned to fly, but they had no chance of escape. The dragon seized one in his jaws, struck down another with his curved talons, and with a single sweep of his great tail broke the backs of the rest.

Then he crouched down beside the murdered man and did not cease to guard him until the people of Macedon came to pay the last funeral dues to their beloved king.

Pindus was buried with all honour in a splendid tomb high on the slopes of the mountains which have ever afterwards born his name.

Then only did the dragon turn and vanish from sight in the deep gorge that led to his cave in the Pindus Mountains.

The Fox and the Dragon

A fox was digging himself a den one day, and he made his earth so deep that he broke through into a great cave in the mountain side.

In the cave he found a large dragon sitting on guard over a great heap of treasure, as is the custom of dragons.

"I beg your pardon for breaking into your home like this," said the fox politely. "Believe me, it was done quite by accident as I dug my earth in the soil of the mountain side. Now I will leave you in peace and fill up the hole which leads into your cave when I go back through it—for treasures of gold and jewels are of no use to a fox. But do tell me—I ask out of simple curiosity—what profit do you get from this dreary toil of keeping guard day and night over this treasure, never getting a wink of sleep or even so much as an afternoon's holiday?"

"No reward at all," answered the dragon. "I guard the treasure because, by the will of Zeus, king of the gods, I have always done so!"

"You mean to say that you never use any of the treasure yourself nor give any of it away to others?" asked the fox.

"No," answered the dragon, "for fate wills that I must guard it—just as all other dragons do."

"Don't be angry if I tell you what I think," remarked the fox, backing out of the cave, "but it strikes me that you and those like you must be suffering under a curse set upon you by Zeus and the gods for some crime you have committed. In the world of men there are a few like you who hoard up all their gold, never get any pleasure out of life and never give any to another human being. They are called misers, and are regarded with nothing but pity and contempt. I feel just that for you. Goodbye!"

With that the fox retreated hastily, put a stone over the hole, and left the dragon to sit on its useless treasure for the rest of its life.

The Dragon and the Peasant

A young dragon was caught in a river flood and stranded on a dry ridge in the bed of the stream when the water sank, unable to fly away having been injured by a floating log. As he sat there wondering what to do, a peasant came down with his donkey to collect drift-wood left by the flood.

"Help me out of this," said the dragon, "and I will bring you wealth."

"How do I know that instead of a reward you will not tear me to pieces as soon as we are out of the river?" said the peasant.

"Tie me up firmly and put me on the back of your donkey," suggested the dragon. "Then I could do you no harm. But indeed I wish you only good fortune—silver and gold, of which I have a good store."

So the peasant tied up the young dragon firmly, hoisted him on to his donkey, and took him to his home not far away.

By the time they got there the peasant was so charmed by the dragon's gentleness—and his promises of treasure—that he lifted him down from the donkey and unfastened the rope with which he had bound him.

"And now," said the peasant, rubbing his hands greedily, "now for the reward of gold and silver that you promised me!"

"Gold and silver?" snorted the dragon, stretching his claws and arching his back to see that all was well with him. "You tie me up so tightly that it hurts—and then you demand gold and silver!"

"But you told me to tie you up!" objected the peasant anxiously.

"Yes, but you tied me up much too tight!" said the dragon. "And now I am going to eat you as a reward!"

The peasant protested at this, begging and praying for his life, and while the argument was going on, a wise fox passed by.

"Hallo!" said the fox. "What is happening here?"

When he heard the story, the fox said to the peasant: "It was very foolish of you to tie up the dragon. But the point is, how did you tie him? If you show me that, I'll be able to judge your case properly."

The dragon agreed to this, and when the peasant had tied him up once more, the fox said:

"Did he bind you as tightly as this before?"

"Oh, much tighter," said the dragon. "So tightly that it really hurt."

"Let me see how you managed that," said the fox, and the peasant tightened the rope round the dragon until it could scarcely breathe.

"Now," said the fox briskly. "Put the dragon on your donkey and take him back to where you found him. Leave him there, still tied up—and then he won't be able to eat you."

And the peasant did just that.

The Dragon's Egg

ONCE there were a man and a dragon who made friends, and lived together like brothers, trusting each other in everything.

The dragon had gathered together a huge treasure of silver and gold, and the time came when he had to go on a journey, and left the man to guard his treasure.

Now this dragon was a wise creature, and he knew what the desire for gold does even to the best of men. He was not sure whether he could quite trust his friend, so he decided to test him.

He brought out an egg in a golden casket and said to the man:

"While I am away I know that you will guard my treasure faithfully, and so I am going to tell you a secret. All my treasure is worth nothing compared with this egg. For on this egg depends my very life. If the egg is broken, I shall die immediately. Therefore guard it with your own life, if you love me."

"I will indeed die before any harm shall come to you, beloved friend," said the man.

So the dragon shut the casket, put it carefully with the rest of his treasure, and went away into a distant country.

After a while the temptation to possess so much gold and silver grew stronger and stronger, until the man could resist it no more.

"Dragons do not know what to do with treasure," he said to himself. "They just collect it and guard it like misers. Now I would be able to spend it properly. . . . All I have to do is to break the magic egg, the dragon will die immediately—and the treasure will be mine."

So the man broke the egg, and took possession of the treasure.

But in fact the dragon had not gone very far away. Suddenly he returned, found that the man had broken the egg—and realized just how trustworthy his friend really was.

And it seems more than likely that the dragon ate the man for his supper that very night.

Dragons and Elephants

THE ancient Greeks and Romans had no doubt at all about the actual existence of dragons, and were already telling stories about them, as we have seen. They even knew about their strange love of collecting gold and guarding it in caves—without any special reason except, as Phaedrus made the dragon say in his version of the old Greek fable:

"I guard my gold for no reason of reward or gain, but because great Zeus has made this the proper employment for dragons."

Another Greek writer, one of the earliest of art critics, Philostratus, described a picture in which there was a hill "encircled by the sea, which is the home of a dragon, guardian doubtless of some rich treasure that lies hidden under the earth. This creature is said to be devoted to gold and whatever golden thing it sees it loves and cherishes; thus the Fleece in Colchis and the Apples of the Hesperides, since they seemed to be of gold, two dragons that never slept guarded and claimed as their own."

The idea of dragons guarding gold may have come from the north by way of the tales of the gryphons whose gold the Arimaspians stole, according to the Greek historian Herodotus, who wrote about 450 B.C. These gryphons were like dragons without a tail, being pictured frequently in Greek art—in sculptures and on vases—as huge lions with the wings of an eagle.

"The northern parts of Europe are very much richer in gold than any other region," says Herodotus. "The story runs that the one-eyed Arimaspians purloin it from the gryphons"; and elsewhere he calls them "the gold-guarding gryphons".

Herodotus believed in the gryphons—though not that the Arimaspians were born with only one eye. And later writers believed even more amazing things about the great serpent-like dragons of India and Africa.

Many reports and stories of these dragons were collected by the Roman writer Pliny (who was killed in the eruption of Vesuvius that buried Pompeii in A.D. 79) and digested into his huge *Natural History*.

Here is what he says about dragons and elephants, in the Elizabethan translation by Philemon Holland, which Shakespeare must have read:

"Elephants breed in that part of Africa which lieth beyond the deserts and wilderness of the Syrtes . . . but India bringeth forth the biggest—as also the dragons that are continually at variance with them, and evermore fighting—and those of such greatness that they can easily clasp and wind round about the elephants, and withal tie them fast with a knot. In this conflict they die, both the one and the other: the elephant he falls down dead as conquered, and with his heavy weight crusheth and squeezeth the dragon that is wound and wreathed about him. . . .

"The dragon therefore, espying the elephant, assaileth him from an high tree and launcheth himself upon him. But the elephant, knowing well enough he is not able to withstand his windings and knittings about him, seeketh to come close to some trees or hard rocks, and so for to crush and squeeze the dragon between him and them. The dragons, ware thereof, entangle and snarl his feet and legs first with their tails. The elephants on the other side undo those knots with their trunks as with a hand; but to prevent that again, the dragons put in their heads into their nostrils and so stop their breathing, and withal fret and gnaw the tenderest parts they find there.

"Now if these two mortal enemies chance to encounter on the way, they bristle and bridle one against another, and prepare themselves to fight: but the chiefest thing the dragons make at is the eye—whereby it comes to pass that many times the elephants are found blind, pined of hunger and worn away. . . .

"Some report of this mortal war between them that the occasion thereof ariseth from a natural cause: for (they say) the elephants' blood is exceeding cold, and therefore the dragons be wonderful desirous thereof to refresh and cool themselves therewith during the parching hot season of the year. And to this purpose they lie under the water, waiting their time to take the elephants at a vantage when they are drinking. They catch fast hold first of their trunk, and they have not so soon clasped and entangled it with their tail, but they set their venomous teeth in the elephant's ear (the only part of all their body which they cannot reach unto with their trunk) and so bite it hard. Now the dragons are so big withal that they are able to receive all the elephant's blood. Thus they are sucked dry until they fall down dead; and the dragons also, drunk with their blood, are squeezed under them and so die together."

Pliny may have thought of dragons as being without wings, but another Roman writer, Lucan, who died only a

few years before him, leaves no doubt of the general belief:

"You also, the dragon, shining with golden brightness, deadly with wings, you move high in the air, and following whole herds you burst asunder vast bulls, embracing them with your folds. Nor is the elephant safe through his size; everything you devote to death, and no need have you of venom for a deadly fate."

The dragons of the ancient world were not always feared, however. Some of them were held sacred, such as that of which both a Roman poet contemporary with Pliny, and Aelian, a writer on natural history of two centuries later, tell us.

This sacred dragon lived in a deep underground cave not far from Rome, and could only be fed from above. However, on special days ceremonies were held outside the dragon's cave, and maidens were let down blindfold into it carrying cakes made of honey and barley:

"Maidens, let down for such a rite, grow pale when their hand is trusted unprotected in the dragon's mouth," says the poet Propertius. "He snatches at the delicacies if offered by a maid; the very baskets tremble in their hands; but if the dragon accepts their offering they return and fall on the necks of their parents, and the farmers cry 'We shall have a fruitful year'!"

If, however, the girl is not good and virtuous, Aelian tells us, "the dragon does not touch it, knowing at once that she is impure, and the food she has touched therefore unsuitable for his sacred touch."

The cake falls to the ground, breaks into little pieces, and the ants come and carry it away crumb by crumb. As for the girl whose shame is thus made manifest to all, "she is punished as the law directs," says Aelian grimly.

Another dragon was worshipped at Melita in Egypt, Aelian goes on to tell us. It was unlawful for anyone to see this dragon, who dwelt in a lonely tower where priests came each day to leave milk, honey and cakes for it in golden bowls set on a special table. And each day when they came they found the bowls empty.

"Upon one occasion, a man of noble birth, who was filled with a great curiosity to see the dragon, having entered alone and placed the food, went out. But when the dragon had begun to eat, he flung open the door suddenly and came in again.

"The dragon was much insulted and left immediately. As for the man who had so impiously desired to see him, he did so to his own destruction. For he was immediately seized with madness, rushed out, and having confessed his crime lost the power of speech, and shortly afterwards died."

Yet another dragon, living in a cave in Epirus in north western Greece, was honoured much as the Roman dragon had been. Each year a great feast was held in its honour, and once again a maiden was chosen who went alone and naked into the cave to offer food to the dragon. If it took the food gently from her hands, the people rejoiced since this meant a fertile and fortunate year. But if it snatched it, and drove her out of the cave, there was lamentation throughout all Epirus, and a year of dearth and misfortune was to be expected.

PART TWO

Dragons of the Dark Ages

Sigurd the Dragon-Slayer

IN the days when the gods of Asgard still walked the earth, a young Prince called Sigurd grew up in the court of his stepfather Hialprek, king of the Danes. Sigurd was the last of the race of the Volsungs and was fated to become one of the great heroes of the North; but as a boy he lived almost unknown under the guardianship of Reginn, the master-smith of Hialprek.

The time came, however, when Sigurd began to thirst for adventures and feel that he must go forth in quest of battle and danger to prove himself worthy of the great race of the Volsungs.

Reginn had waited eagerly for this moment, since, although he had brought up Sigurd well and honestly, he was at heart a villain who thought only of his own gain and cared not how he came by it.

As they spoke of mighty deeds one evening, Reginn said: "In a cave on Gnita Heath dwells the Dragon Fafnir, guarding the greatest treasure in all the land of Denmark. But no one dares go near to slay him, for so deadly is the poison which pours from his mouth that no man may endure it and live."

"I will go against Fafnir the Dragon!" cried Sigurd. "But first of all, make me a sword worthy of so great a deed—worthy also to be wielded by the son of Sigmund the son of Volsung the Great!"

"Such a sword will I make," said Reginn, and next morning set to work in his forge. But when the sword was finished, Sigurd struck the anvil with it, and the blade shivered into fragments.

"You must make me a better sword than that, if I am to slay Fafnir!" laughed Sigurd.

Then Reginn put all his knowledge and cunning into the forging of a new blade, and when he brought the sword to him, Sigurd gazed on it with admiration.

"Surely this will satisfy you now," said Reginn, "though you would prove a hard task-master for any smith!"

Again Sigurd tested the sword by smiting the anvil with it, and as before the blade broke into many pieces.

"You are but a poor smith!" cried Sigurd. "Or is it that you wish to betray me to Fafnir the Dragon?"

As Reginn made no answer to this, nor any suggestion as to the making of a stronger sword, Sigurd went to his mother Queen Hiordis and said:

"I have heard it rumoured that when my father King Sigmund was carried dying out of his last and greatest battle, he brought you the good sword Gram which Odin, king of the gods, had given to him."

"That is true," answered the Queen. "But, since he was fated to die in that battle, the sword Gram was broken in two pieces."

"Give me the pieces, I beg of you," said Sigurd, "for I would have a sword made from them that is worthy of the last of the Volsungs."

Queen Hiordis went to her treasure chest and drew from it the two pieces of a mighty sword. She gave them to Sigurd, saying:

"Take them, my son. You are fated to win great fame with the sword Gram." So Sigurd carried the broken blade to Reginn, and the master smith took the two pieces, cursing Sigurd under his breath, and set to work. He put all his great skill into the remaking of Gram, and when it was finished, it seemed as if fire burned along the edges of the blade as he handed it to Sigurd.

Never had there been so fair a sword. Yet Sigurd must needs test it as he had done with the others. But this time when he whirled it aloft and struck the anvil, the keen blade cut through the iron and deep into the wooden stock beneath without so much as blunting its edge.

"This is a fine blade indeed!" cried Sigurd, as he girded the sword Gram to his side. "Now lead me to Gnita Heath so that I may try its worth on the great Dragon Fafnir."

So Sigurd and Reginn rode away into the wilderness and came at length to the river where Fafnir was wont to drink. And there they saw a long trail leading down to the water's side made by the Dragon as he came down from his cave on the Gnita Heath high up the mountain beyond it.

"You told me that the Dragon was no bigger than other worms who guard their treasures in caves of the earth," said Sigurd. "But now that I see his tracks, and the great trench he has made in the rock coming down each day to the water, I would guess that he is by far the greatest of all Dragons."

"You may kill him, none the less," answered Reginn, "if you will but dig yourself a hole in the trench which is the Dragon's path and stab him to the heart as he passes above you on his way down to drink at the river."

"Will not the Dragon's blood burn or poison me if any of it gushes out over me as I stab him?" asked Sigurd.

"What is the use of me offering you advice, if you are afraid of every danger," exclaimed Reginn scornfully.

At this Sigurd strode angrily up the Dragon's path towards the cave. But Reginn made haste to find a hiding place among the rocks by the river, for he was very much afraid.

As Sigurd began to dig himself a pit in the Dragon's path, an old man with a long, white beard who had only one eye under his broad-brimmed hat came up to him suddenly and asked what he was doing.

Sigurd explained the plan, and the old man said: "You are following the advice of one who wishes you evil. Reginn would have you kill the Dragon—but perish in the battle so that he can take all the treasure. What you should do is to dig a deep pit with a shallow trench running out from the side of it, so that you may lie in the trench while the Dragon's blood falls only into the pit after you have stabbed him to the heart with the good sword Gram."

Having said this, the old man vanished mysteriously, and Sigurd realized that it had been none other than Odin, king of the Gods of Asgard, who had spoken to him. For he now remembered to have heard that in the disguise of an old one-eyed man with a broad-brimmed hat and a long cloak Odin was wont to visit those mortals whom he wished to help or protect.

So Sigurd dug the deep pit and the shallow trench, lay down in the latter, and waited for Fafnir the Dragon.

As the sun rose red and angry over the cold, desolate waste, Fafnir came out of his cave and made his way down towards the river for his morning drink. As he came slowly down the mountain side the ground shook beneath his tread and the poison dripped from his jaws.

Sigurd was not frightened by the dreadful roaring of the Dragon nor of the steaming venom. But as the creature passed over the pit he thrust the sword Gram under its left shoulder and up to the very hilt, deep into its heart. Then he plucked out the sword quickly and with the same movement drew back along the trench in which he lay.

As soon as Fafnir realized that he had his death-wound, he lashed out with head and tail so that all things within reach of him were broken to pieces. Then, knowing that his death was upon him, he lay still and spoke with a human voice saying:

"What mighty hero has slain me? What mighty son of a famous father is so bold as to come against me sword in hand?"

Knowing how dangerous a dying curse might be, Sigurd answered:

"Unknown to men is my kin: I am called but a noble beast."

Then Fafnir said: "Reginn has done this, I know full well—Reginn my brother who hates me. For I was a man even as he until I stole the gold, Andvari's Treasure, from him and with it Andvari's magic Ring. Yet it gladdens my heart that he is with you, for I know all that he plans. And now it comes to me that you are Sigurd the Volsung who shall be called Fafnir's Bane for my slaying. Take my gold, Andvari's Hoard, but remember that it will itself be the bane of all who own it even as it has been mine. For the Curse of Andvari the dwarf is upon it."

After this Fafnir rolled upon the ground and died. Yet even in death he did not regain his human form, but remained a Dragon.

Then came Reginn to Sigurd and said: "Hail, mighty hero! You have won a noble victory over the Dragon whom none else dared to face. Yet he was once my brother, and I too am in part guilty of his death. Now let me take the full guilt upon myself so that there may be no

blood-feud between your kin and mine. And this I may
do if you cut out the Dragon's heart, roast it with fire and
give it to me to eat. When this is done all guilt shall be
mine, nor any blame rest on you who have done no more
than slay a dragon."

Sigurd did as Reginn asked, and soon the Dragon's heart
was roasting on a rod before the fire.

After a while Sigurd touched the heart to see if it were yet cooked, and the hot gravy burnt his finger so that he put it quickly to his mouth. The moment the heart's-blood of the Dragon touched his tongue, he straightaway understood the speech of all the birds. And he heard what the woodpeckers in the trees nearby were chattering about:

"There sits Sigurd," said one of them, "roasting the Dragon's heart for another man to eat. If he ate it himself he would become the wisest of all men, and the most fortunate. For we could tell him how to win the lady Brynhild, Odin's daughter, from her magic sleep to be his wife—and how to become a great king too."

"And look," said another bird, "there sits Reginn, planning to murder Sigurd and steal Andvari's Hoard for himself. Yes, and if Reginn eats the Dragon's heart, what is to stop him winning Brynhild instead of Sigurd?"

And a third woodpecker cried: "Why does not Sigurd strike off that traitor Reginn's head and win Andvari's Hoard for himself—and all else that we could tell him of, if only he ate the Dragon's heart?"

"Indeed, why not!" exclaimed Sigurd springing to his feet. "Let Reginn go by the same road as Fafnir his brother!"

As he spoke he whipped out the sword Gram and smote off Reginn's head in an instant. Then he made his supper off the Dragon's heart and spent the night in the cave, sleeping upon Andvari's Hoard, the mighty treasure which Fafnir the Dragon had guarded for so long.

And next day, guided by the birds, Sigurd the Volsung set out to win Brynhild as his wife and to become the greatest of all the ancient heroes of the North.

Beowulf and the Dragon

SOME fifteen hundred years ago a king called Beowulf ruled over the Geats who lived in the south of Sweden. He was a mighty warrior who, as a young man, had done deeds of which the minstrels and poets would tell through after ages. He had come to Denmark where King Hrothgar was sorely troubled by the marsh-monster, Grendel, who came each night when the warriors slept in the great hall called Heorot and carried one off to his den.

Beowulf watched all night in Heorot and when Grendel came he wrestled with him and tore off his arm. Wounded, Grendel slunk back to his pool. But next night Grendel's mother, a monster as grim and terrible as he, came to Heorot and carried off another warrior.

Beowulf followed her to the mere, dived down beneath its dark waters and came up in the fearsome cave under the bank in which the monsters lived. Here he fought and killed Grendel's mother—and in the cave found Grendel dead from the wounds he had received in Heorot.

For these deeds, and others almost as noteworthy, Beo-wulf was known throughout all the North. But his greatest battle was to be his last—his battle with the Dragon that came out to slay his own people of the Geats and lay waste their homes.

It chanced that a warrior, one of Beowulf's own thanes,

a knight of his court, was attacked by a band of enemies too numerous for him to fight alone. So he fled from them up into the mountains, trying vainly to find some hiding-place. They were close behind him, and escape seemed impossible, when at last he found a cave well hidden among the rocks. Into this he went, and, crouching down in a dark corner, heard his enemies go by. But he dared not venture out in case they were lying in wait for him. So presently he went deeper into the cave—and was surprised to see a dull gleam of light ahead.

Further he went, and then paused in amazement. The cave opened out into a great cavern, and in the middle of it was a huge heap of treasure—gold and jewels, engraved bowls and helmets, jewelled brooches and shining swords and shields. A mysterious light shone dimly over this piled treasure, and to his horror the thane saw a huge Dragon sleeping above the gold, the fire flickering from his nostrils.

Then he was minded to turn and flee quickly and softly away. But the lure of the gold was too much for him. Very quietly he took off his cloak and gathered into it as many rings and jewels and golden cups and bowls as he could easily carry. Then, and only then, did he tiptoe out of the cave and hasten away over the mountains to his own farmstead.

Next day he buried most of the treasure under the floor, but one golden cup he took to Beowulf, saying simply that he had found it in a cave on the mountains.

But very soon his theft brought disaster upon the people of the Geats. For the following night the Dragon woke from a long sleep and at once realized that he had been robbed: for he knew each piece of treasure, and saw at once that some had gone.

This Dragon—"the old twilight foe, the naked hostile
dragon, who seeks barrows of the dead, flaming as he goes,
who flies by night compassed with fire"—had found that
treasure in the ancient pagan days, had gathered it into the
cavern and guarded it there for three hundred years.

When he knew that he had been robbed, the Dragon
grew mad with rage. Out of the cave he rushed, found the

thane's footprints, knew that a man had come into his cavern, and set out to wreak vengeance.

"The monster began to pour flames out of his mouth, to burn the bright dwellings. The flare of the fire brought fear upon men. The loathsome flier did not wish to leave one of them alive. The warring of the Dragon was widely seen, the onslaught of the cruel foe far and near, how the enemy of the people of the Geats wrought despite and devastation. He hastened back to his hoard, to his hideous hall, before day came. But he had harassed the dwellers in the land with fire, with flames and destruction. Now he trusted to be safe in his cavern, safe because of his fearsome strength. But his hope deceived him."

Quickly the terror that had come upon them was made known to Beowulf by his people. And Beowulf at once realized that his thane had stolen the goblet from the Dragon's hoard, and doubtless much treasure besides—and that there was no way in which to make peace with the Dragon.

So he prepared for what he feared might well be his last battle. First he bade his smiths make him a great shield of iron, for well he knew that the usual shield of linden-wood had no chance against the fiery breath of the Dragon. Then he put on his helmet and armour, girded his sword and his battle-knife at his side, and called together his thanes and warriors.

When they were gathered he said: "I go now alone to fight against the Dragon, I who in younger days slew Grendel the terrible marsh-stepper and the monster his mother; I who wrestled with Brecca the strong-swimmer all a winter's day; I who have fought and won in many a battle of men when Hygelac my uncle ruled the Geats. If I could prevail without a sword, no sword would I carry.

But I cannot fight a Dragon as I fought Grendel—for I expect hot battle-flame and a blast of poisoned breath. Therefore I go fully armed, bearing a shield of iron. But this I vow: not one step backwards will I take once I raise my sword against the Dragon: where we meet, there will I fight to the death."

Then Beowulf set out for the Dragon's cave. His warriors followed him, but remained at a distance to see the battle.

Beowulf strode up to the cave entrance and cried his defiance in a loud voice. Hearing him, hate welled up in the heart of the Dragon. Out of the cave poured flames, the hot battle-breath of the monster, and the Dragon came, lashing his tail in fury.

Forward went Beowulf holding his shield before him, his ancient sword bare in his hand, and the flames curled round him. "The lord of the Geats raised up his hand, he struck the dreadful gleaming monster with the precious sword so that the bright edge turned on the bone; it bit less keenly than its King, hard-pressed by trouble, had need. After that battle-stroke the guardian of the treasure was in a savage mood; he poured forth deadly fire, the war-flames leapt far. Beowulf, friend of the Geats, uttered no battle-boasts of former victories, for the bare battle-blade had failed him in dire need, the long-famous brand. It was no easy thing for so great a warrior to step back—yet so must any man do at need.

"It was not long ere the fighters closed once more. The treasure-guardian took new heart, his breast laboured with breathing—and Beowulf suffered anguish, ringed round with fire. Nor did his followers stand by any longer to watch the battle; instead they ran for the wood, they hid to save their lives."

But one of them was stirred with shame, felt his heart leap with the desire to achieve mighty deeds. His name was Wiglaf, a young warrior distantly related to Beowulf, not yet tried in battle, though he bore his father's sword and shield which had come victorious out of many battles.

"Wiglaf's spirit did not weaken, nor did his father's sword fail in the fight. That the Dragon discovered on their first meeting.

"But ere he rushed upon his foe he spoke to the warriors who had fled: 'Let us go to the help of our warlike King while the fierce dread flame still flares. God knows I would think it shame to see him enveloped in that fire and not go to share the danger with him. It does not seem to me right that any of us should bear our shields back to our homes if we do not first fell the foe, guard the life of the guardian of the Geats.'

"Forward then he went through the deadly smoke, went armed to the aid of his king, and spoke but few words: 'Beowulf, beloved of us all, triumph in this battle as in the days of your youth you swore to triumph and win fame while your life lasted—now, resolute warrior, mighty in deeds, thou must guard thy life with all thy strength, and I will help thee!'

"At these words the Dragon came raging once more, the dread evil creature, flashing with surges of flame to seek his enemies, the men whom he hated. Wiglaf's shield withered in the fire till but the rim remained; nor did the corselet on his chest give much protection to the young warrior. But he fought mightily, sheltering behind Beowulf's shield after his own was consumed by the fiery breath.

"Then again warlike Beowulf bethought him of his fame as a warrior: he struck with his battle-sword with all his might—struck with Naegling that ancient blade that had won so many battles in earlier days. But the old grey steel failed in this fight: he smote too hard and the sword shivered into pieces. . . . Now was he in evil plight.

"Then for the third time that enemy of mankind, that flaming Dragon, ravened for battle. He rushed on the mighty warrior when he saw his chance and, hot and fierce in fight, he bit into his neck and shoulder with his sharp teeth. Then Beowulf was stained with his life-blood, the gore welled.

"Then Wiglaf, seeing the deadly peril of his prince, showed the great courage and daring that was in him. Not pausing to guard his head, he lashed out bravely with his sword, so strongly that it sank deep into the Dragon's body, in spite of all his scales. And at that the flames pouring from the Dragon's mouth, grew less.

"Then once more Beowulf the great king was himself again. He drew his keen and battle-sharp knife which he wore in his corselet, and he plunged it deep into the Dragon's belly. Then the foe fell; force drove out his life." Beowulf finished what Wiglaf had begun, and the Dragon sank down and died.

"That was the last victory of Beowulf the mighty warrior, the end of his work in this world. The wound which the Dragon had given him began to burn and swell: right soon he found that the poison was working with deadly force in his body." He staggered to a rock outside the cave and sank on to it.

Beowulf sat there a while and spoke to Wiglaf, telling him that his death was near, speaking of all he had done for the people of the Geats during the fifty years of his reign, saying that he went to meet his Maker without fear.

Presently he spoke again: "Now that the Dragon lies

dead, smitten with deep wounds, so, dear Wiglaf, hasten into his cave and bring out the treasure, the riches of olden times, so that I may gaze on the bright gems and the gold-smith's artful work, and for that sight pass away more easily from life, and from the land which I have guarded for so long."

Then Wiglaf went into the cave and carried out great armfuls of treasure: helmets and swords and shields; rings, bracelets, and chains of gold; cups, bowls and platters inlaid with jewels; jewel-encrusted brooches and girdles and combs—all these he carried out of the cave and piled in a great heap before the dying king.

"Beowulf spoke again, the dying hero gazing on the gold: 'I give thanks aloud to the Prince, the King of Glory, the Eternal Lord for all that I see here, all the great treasure that I have been able to win for my people on this my death-day. I have here given my waning life for this heap of treasure: spend it well, for the good of my people, you who must guard them now. For I may tarry no longer in this world. When I am dead bid the warriors raise a great mound over my ashes at the sea-headland. Let it tower high on Hronesness, a reminder to my people, so that for ever after men at sea may call it 'Beowulf's Barrow' when they see it from their tall ships as they sail by.'

"The dying king took his ring and gave it to Wiglaf. He took his helmet bright with gold from his head and gave him that also, bidding him use them well.

" 'Thou art the last of our line,' he said. 'Fate has swept all away and I must needs follow them. I have no son to whom I may give my ring and my helmet: be you the guardian of the Geats.'

"Those were Beowulf's last words, his last thoughts ere his body was ready for the funeral pyre. As he spoke them his soul passed from his breast to seek the glory of Heaven.

"Great sorrow fell upon Wiglaf when he saw the man he loved best lying dead on the ground, his life ended. But the slayer also lay still, the dreadful Dragon of the earth, bereft of life, vanquished by the valiant. No longer could the coiling Dragon keep guard over the hoards of treasure, but swords and knife had laid him low so that he lay dead beside his cave, never to fly again. No more would he wheel in his flight through the air at midnight, nor gather treasure into his cave." Beowulf had slain the Dragon, won the treasure for his people, and died doing his mightiest deed.

Ragnar Shaggy-Legs and the Dragons

MORE than two hundred years after the death of Beowulf there was a king of Sweden called Herodd who, when hunting in the woods one day, caught two baby dragons and brought them back to his hall as playthings for his daughter Thora.

This was a foolish thing to do, and it was not long before Herodd and his people were regretting it bitterly. For the dragons grew at a prodigious rate, and very soon needed the carcase of a whole ox each for a single day's food. And then they broke out of captivity, settled themselves in a cave in the nearby mountains, and began to ravage the countryside, withering it up with their venomous breath. Unlike most dragons these did not breath fire, but their breath was so poisonous that it shrivelled up all living things.

At this, King Herodd repented of his foolishness in bringing the dragons alive to his court, and proclaimed that whoever killed them should marry his daughter the Princess Thora and be king after him.

Many warriors came to try their strength against the dragons, attracted by the chance of winning fame and the princess. But some fled, and others died from the dragons' venom.

Now Ragnar, prince of Denmark, had fallen in love with Thora; and when he heard about King Herodd's offer, he decided to win both her and the kingdom. So, after much thought, he had a suit of clothes made for him of wool stuffed with hair, and he prepared leggings of goat skin that came up to his waist, sewn with hairy side outwards. Then he set off for Sweden, and as soon as he landed deliberately plunged his whole body into water and then stayed out all night during a hard frost so that his whole strange costume was frozen, like armour made out of ice. Then he tied his sword to his side, lashed his spear to his arm with a thong, and set out for where the dragons were.

Herodd's courtiers came out to see the battle: but when the two dragons appeared and charged the strange figure of Ragnar, all fled, shrieking like frightened little girls. Meanwhile the dragons were trying to kill Ragnar, sometimes striking at him with their mighty tails, and sometimes pouring poison over him from their terrible jaws, until even King Herodd followed his courtiers into hiding.

But Ragnar, trusting in his armour of frozen wool and the hardness of his clothes, foiled the poisonous assaults not only with his weapons, but with his very attire, and, single-handed, in unwearying combat, stood up against the two gaping dragons, who stubbornly poured forth their venom upon him. For their teeth he repelled with his shield, their poison with his dress.

At last he hurled his spear and drove it against the bodies of the brutes who were attacking him so hard. His aim was strong and true—for he had waited until the perfect moment—and the spear passed through both their hearts, and they sank down dead, leaving him victor.

By the time King Herodd and his courtiers came out to view the bodies of the dead dragons and congratulate the conqueror, Ragnar's clothes were no longer frozen, and

he presented a very strange, shaggy sight—particularly from the waist downwards, where the matted hair of the mountain goats added to his grotesque appearance.

At once King Herodd gave him the nickname of "Shaggy-legs" in memory of his great battle with the dragons, and Ragnar Lodbrog—Ragnar Shaggy-legs—was celebrated in song and saga throughout the North.

An Adventure of Digenes the Borderer

DURING the ninth century, when the Emperor of Byzantium still ruled what had been the Roman Empire and was lord over all the lands from the Adriatic to the Caspian Sea, there lived a great warrior called Digenes Akrites.

His second name meant "Borderer", for he guarded the eastern border of the Empire, keeping the Moslems out of the Christian domains of the Emperor of Byzantium.

He had many adventures, during which he captured the beautiful Greek girl Evdokia to be his wife and the companion of his wanderings in his never-ending guardianship of the Emperor's domains.

One beautiful spring day, when the earth was green with fresh grass and bright with flowers, they rested beside the River Euphrates, far up near its source on the borders of Armenia.

Digenes had lain down to sleep in his tent during the heat of midday, and Evdokia, being thirsty went down to the river for a drink.

She sat on the bank, dabbling her feet in the water, the fairest girl in all the land—the rose seeming to bloom in her cheeks, her lips parting like the opening bud of a fair flower, and her golden curls shining like the sunlight on her brow. To see her was to experience joy unspeakable.

So thought a Dragon whose home was by the stream.

He had the power of shape-shifting, and now he turned himself into a handsome young man and came towards her among the flowers, saying:

"Lovely maiden, be mine and I will give you all this fair land and riches beyond your dreams."

But Evdokia knew him for what he was, and answered:

"Dragon, you plot in vain. Give up your wicked plan. I am not deceived—I know you by your eyes. Beware! He who guards me does but sleep, and is nearby. If he wakens and finds you here, he will do you grievous hurt."

The Dragon was not put off, however. With a cry of triumph he leapt forward, seized Evdokia in his arms, and turned to carry her away.

But Evdokia cried out: "Digenes, awake! Come to the aid of your love!"

The voice struck to the heart of Digenes who woke on the instant, and on the next came bounding out of his tent, sword ready in his hand.

He saw the beautiful young man holding the struggling Evdokia in his arms, and his feet were like wings as he raced down the bank.

There was no escape for the thief, who dropped Evdokia, turned to meet Digenes, and in a moment had assumed his own proper form.

Many a man might have turned in terror from that dreadful shape. A three-headed Dragon it was, flames of fire gushing from each mouth. Roaring, it sprang to meet Digenes, the earth shaking at the sound and the trees bending as if struck by a gale of wind.

Now the three great heads of the Dragon grew each from a separate neck. But the necks joined just before they met the body which was of great thickness until it tapered away in the long coiling tail.

As the Dragon leapt upon him, Digenes sprang to one side and struck a single blow with his long, keen sword—straight at the single neck below the three heads. So strongly did he smite and so sharp was the blade that he cut the neck right through. The three heads fell together, and the Dragon rolled over, lashing its tail for the last time, and lay still.

Digenes calmly wiped his sword and returned it to its sheath. Then he shouted for his servants to take away the Dragon, kissed Evdokia, and went back to his tent to finish his interrupted sleep before his next adventure.

The Red Dragon of Wales

IN the days before Caesar conquered Britain there lived a king called Lludd who built himself a city in the south-east of the island, set about it a wall with towers and gates, and named it after himself, Caer Lludd—which the Romans called Londinium and the Saxons London. And in today's city Ludgate is still called after that ancient king.

Lludd ruled peacefully for many years. But not long before the first coming of the Romans many strange evils fell upon the land: and among them was "a shriek that came on every May-eve, over every hearth in the Island of Britain. And this went through people's hearts, and so scared them, that the men lost their hue and their strength, and the woman their children, and the young men and the maidens lost their senses, and all the animals and trees and the earth and the waters were left barren.

"And thereupon King Lludd felt great sorrow and care, because he knew not how he might be freed from this plague. And he called to him all the nobles of his kingdom, and asked counsel of them what they should do against this affliction. And by the common counsel of the nobles, Lludd the son of Beli went to Llevelys his brother, king of France, for he was a man of great counsel and wisdom, to seek his advice."

King Llevelys was indeed wise beyond all men living at

that time. For after a little he was able to tell his brother both the cause of that terrible shriek, and how he might set free the Island of Britain from it.

"This plague that is in your kingdom," said Llevelys, "is caused by a red dragon. Another dragon of a foreign race is fighting with it, and striving to overcome it. And therefore does your dragon make a fearful outcry. And in this wise may you overcome the plague. After you have returned home, command that the Island be measured in its length and breadth, and in the place where you find its exact central point, have a pit dug, and command a cauldron full of the best mead that can be made to be put in the pit, with a covering of satin over the face of the cauldron. And then remain watching, and you will see the dragons fighting—first in the shape of other animals, and then as flying dragons battling in the air. Finally, after wearying themselves with fierce and furious fighting, they will fall upon the covering, and they will sink in, and the covering with them, and they will draw it down to the very bottom of the cauldron. And they will drink up the whole of the mead; and after that they will sleep. Thereupon do you immediately fold the covering around them, and bury them in two stone chests, in the strongest place you have in your dominions, and heap earth over them."

Then Lludd returned back to his own land. And he "caused the Island of Britain to be measured in its length and in its breadth. And in Oxford he found the central point, and in that place he caused the earth to be dug, and in that pit a cauldron to be set, full of the best mead that could be made, and a covering of satin over the face of it. And he himself watched that night. And while he was there, he beheld the dragons fighting. And when they were weary they fell, and came down upon the top of the satin, and drew it with them to the bottom of the cauldron. And when they had drunk the mead they slept. And in their sleep, Lludd folded the covering around them, and in the securest place he had in Snowdon he hid them, in two stone chests. Now after that the place was called Dinas Emrys, but before that, Dinas Ffaraon. And thus the fierce outcry ceased in his kingdom."

Five centuries later, after the Romans had conquered Britain, and occupied it for more than four hundred years, and left it as the Saxon invaders began to pour in from the east, and Picts to flood over Hadrian's Wall to the north, a king called Vortigern ruled the Island.

In trying to beat back the invaders he made the great mistake of inviting other Saxons under their chieftains Hengest and Horsa to come to his aid, granting them part of the country in return. For very soon they were demanding more and more, and it seemed that before long they would conquer the whole Island of Britain.

Driven at length into the mountains of North Wales, Vortigern sought out a strong place on which to build a castle that would withstand any attacks from the Saxons. He consulted his twelve wise men, and they all advised the great mound at the foot of Snowdon by Nant Gwynant called Dinas Emrys.

On top of Dinas Emrys there is a wide, flat shelf covering half the summit, and behind it a curved rocky ridge suitable for the towers of a castle. On the wide shelf of flat ground Vortigern bade his stone-masons and carpenters build him a hall with many rooms round about it, and walls with towers outside that again.

So hewn stones and shaped timbers were carried up Dinas Emrys and stacked ready for building the hall. But next morning they had all disappeared and nothing remained with which to begin constructing the great castle of refuge, nor even the hall that was to be its centre.

Materials were at once collected for a second time and stacked ready for use. But a second time they vanished in the night as if the soft green turf in the centre of the place had opened and swallowed them up.

Then Vortigern consulted his wise men, and they said: "You must find a child born without a father, put him to death and sprinkle his blood on the ground where the hall is to be built—otherwise you will never accomplish your purpose."

So Vortigern sent messengers throughout Britain, and in Monmouth they came upon a boy whose mother swore that he had no father—save only one who had visited her in a dream and seemed to be no earthly man.

They brought the boy to Vortigern where he sat on a rock on Dinas Emrys, and stood him before the king on the flat space where the turf seemed to grow much greener than elsewhere.

"Why have you brought me here?" asked the boy.

"My wise men have said that only if the stones are cemented with your blood can my hall be built in this place," answered Vortigern.

"By what magic do you know this?" the boy asked of the wise men. "For I think it is by magic that you have sought to find how the stones and timbers may be stopped from vanishing each night in the ground."

But the wise men answered nothing, and they were afraid of the boy's knowledge.

"My lord king," said the boy, "let me prove to you the ignorance of these men, and that even I can see further and more clearly than they. Bid them answer the questions that I put to them."

"Answer what he asks," said Vortigern shortly.

"First," said the boy, "tell me what lies hidden under this place that will not let any building be erected upon it."

When they could not answer, the boy said: "I beg your majesty to command your workmen to dig into the ground, and you will find a pool of water which causes the foundations to sink and the materials to be swallowed up."

This was done, and presently they uncovered a deep pool under the ground which had caused the earth to give way beneath the stones and beams.

"Now tell me what lies at the bottom of this pool," said the boy. And when the wise men could not answer, he said: "At the bottom lie two chests made of stone. I beg your majesty to have the pool drained, and you shall see them."

When the pool was drained the two stone chests stood revealed, and the boy said: "Tell me now what lies hidden inside them. . . . You cannot, then I will do so. In one chest is imprisoned a Red Dragon and in the other a White Dragon. Open, and you shall see if I speak truth."

As soon as the two chests were opened the two Dragons whom King Lludd had imprisoned there awoke from sleep and came out. And one of them was red and the other white. Immediately they saw one another they charged screaming and hissing, and a terrible battle began, with flames pouring from their mouths and the smoke half-hiding them from view.

Soon the White Dragon seemed to be winning, and it chased the Red Dragon which fled with terrible shrieks to the edge of the hill of Dinas Emrys, and flew round and round it, pursued by its adversary.

But presently the Red Dragon turned at bay, and in a

little while it was chasing the White Dragon: and at length
the White Dragon flew screaming away up towards the
top of Snowdon. And the last they saw of them was the
Red Dragon prancing in triumph on the very summit of
the mountain, before the clouds came down and hid him
from their sight.

Then said the boy: "The Red Dragon signifies our people
of Britain. For a long time he shall suffer woe and be
driven into hiding by the White Dragon, who signifies the
Saxons whom you have invited into the Island. For a little
space the Red Dragon shall conquer, when King Arthur
rules this land: but when he passes into Avalon, the White
Dragon shall triumph wholely, and the Saxons shall rule
all Britain. Yet at the last Arthur shall return, and the Red
Dragon of Wales conquer the White and set his country
free."

There was a long silence of awe when the boy finished
speaking. At last King Vortigern said:

"It seems to me that you are a greater magician and a
wiser man, boy though you are, than any of these who
think to advise me. Tell us now, what is your name?"

"I am Merlin," was the answer, "Merlin, whose name is
also Emrys. And Dinas Emrys is the place where I shall
dwell. Dinas Emrys which is "Merlin's Castle"—and here
I shall lie hid until the time comes when I am needed."

After this Vortigern and his followers departed from
Dinas Emrys, and before long the Saxons triumphed over
him and he was burnt to ashes in the castle of refuge which
he built for himself at Gwent in Monmouthshire.

But when Uther Pendragon ruled over Britain (albeit
the Saxons held most of the land) Merlin led him by night
to the castle of dark Tintagel by the Cornish sea. And there
the lady Ygraine bore him a son called Arthur, whom

Merlin hid until the day came when he was to draw the Sword Excalibur from the stone and become king of the Island of Britain and, with his Knights of the Round Table, drive back the Saxons and free the country from them for one bright generation—before the darkness fell again.

Sir Tristram in Ireland

IN the days when King Arthur ruled Britain there was a young knight of Cornwall called Tristram of Lyonesse—who was destined one day to sit at his Round Table.

While still unknown in Camelot, he had gained great fame by killing in single-combat Sir Marhault, champion of Gurman, King of Ireland, and so freeing Cornwall from paying a cruel tribute each year of youths and maidens.

Tristram was wounded in the fight, and as Marhault's sword was poisoned the wound could not be cured until he went disguised as the minstrel Tramtris to the very court of King Gurman whose wife Queen Isaud was skilled in the making of poisons and potions.

In his disguise he became a welcome guest, for he could play the harp and sing more sweetly than any other minstrel in Ireland. And he knew lays of brave knights and fair ladies, of perilous quests and enchanted castles that could hold his hearers spell-bound far into the night.

When at last he returned to his uncle King Mark of Cornwall he told, among other things, of the beauty of Princess Iseult, daughter of King Gurman and Queen Isaud.

Then King Mark held council with his lords and said: "King Gurman has no other child: would it not be well for both our lands if I made a lasting peace by taking the fair Iseult to be my wife and the Queen of Cornwall?"

This seemed a wise plan. "But how can this happen?" they asked. "The King and Queen of Ireland hate us for the slaying of Marhault and the ending of the tribute. How then may you win the hand of Iseult in marriage?"

Then spoke Tristram: "My uncle, and you lords of Cornwall, I will adventure this difficult and dangerous quest. I have been once into Ireland and won the friendship of the fair Iseult and the Queen her mother, who cured me of my wound—though they had vowed vengeance to the death on Tristram of Lyonesse!"

So Tristram, who already had a plan in his mind for winning the fair Iseult, set out secretly in one small ship, came to Ireland, and anchored in a quiet haven. Then, leaving his second in command to guard the ship, with instructions to pass it off as a vessel from Britain engaged in trade, he went on shore at dead of night, fully armed.

For Tristram knew that there was a dragon in Ireland, a fearful monster which devoured the people and laid waste the land; and he knew that King Gurman had promised that whoever could slay the dragon should marry his daughter Iseult. So he set out for the dragon's lair high up among the burnt rocks above a fire-scorched valley in the dark mountains near where he had moored his ship.

Early next morning, when the red rays of the rising sun slanted down the valley like the blood which the dragon had shed dripping and pouring over the rocks, Tristram saw three knights, and a man who followed them secretly as if not wishing to be seen by them, ride over the pass and down towards the lair of the dragon.

Presently he heard the dragon roar, and there came the cries of men in mortal anguish, and an evil smoke curled up over the rocks. Then the man who had followed the three knights came galloping back the way he had come, spurring his horse to make it go faster. Now this was the Seneschal of King Gurman, a cowardly knight and a braggart, who dared not face the dragon, yet boasted that he had often ridden to seek it: for his heart was set on winning the fair Iseult—and with her the kingdom.

Tristram thought no more of him, but rode softly down into the valley, and presently saw the dragon standing over one of the knights whom it had slain. A terrible monster it was, with great shining claws, scales of blue and green, and jaws breathing fire and smoke between sharp white teeth.

Then Tristram set his spear in rest and charged the dragon suddenly, his shield held well before him, and the monster turned at the sound of hooves and made ready to seize him with open jaws. Right well aimed Sir Tristram, so that the spear entered the dragon's mouth and pierced deep towards its heart.

Tristram leapt forward over the dragon's head; and the monster, screaming with rage and pain, slew the horse in a blast of fire and began to devour it. But the spear, though the wooden handle charred swiftly to ashes, left its long, sharp point deep in the creature's vitals, and it went screaming away into the rocky ravine that led to its cave, leaving the horse half eaten.

Tristram followed after the dragon, which fled before him roaring for pain till the rocks rang and re-echoed with the sound. It spurted fire from its jaws and tore up the earth on either side, till the pain of its internal wound overcame it, and it turned and crouched down under a wall of rock.

Then Tristram drew his sword, thinking to slay the monster easily, but it was a hard battle, the hardest he had

ever fought, and in truth he did not think to survive it. For the dragon brought against him smoke and flame, teeth and claws sharper than any razor; and Tristram found it hard to shelter behind trees and rocks, for the fight was so fierce that the shield he held on his arm was all twisted with the heat and well-nigh melted away.

But the battle came to a sudden end. The spear-point in the dragon's vitals worked its way towards the creature's heart so that it flung itself on the ground, rolling over and over in agony.

Then Tristram leapt forward swiftly and smote with his sword to the very heart of the monster, so deeply that the blade went in right to the hilt. Then the dragon let out a roar so grim and terrible that it sounded as if heaven and earth were falling together; and that death cry was heard far and wide through the land.

Tristram himself trembled with horror and with weakness. But, seeing that the dragon was dead, he went near and with much difficulty forced open its jaws, cut out the tongue, and hid it safely in the pouch on his belt. Then he staggered away into the desolation that surrounded the dragon's lair, thinking to rest during the day and return to his ship under cover of darkness. But he was so overcome by the fight and the fiery breath of the dragon that he was almost exhausted. Seeing a pool of clear water with a spring welling from a rock beside it, he staggered to its edge. But as he bent down, the weight of his armour and the venom of the dragon overcame him, and he fell senseless by the spring.

Meanwhile the Seneschal, who would fain be the princess's husband, as he rode homeward heard the death-cry of the dragon.

"Ah-ha!" said he to himself. "Someone has slain or

mortally wounded the dragon. With cunning and good luck I may still succeed!"

So he rode back, and presently found the remains of Tristram's horse. At this he paused, shaking with fear. But presently, as he heard no sound, he rode fearfully along the track to the dragon's cave and came suddenly upon the creature itself lying dead. He was so terrified by the sight that he fell off his horse and began to run. But as he found that the dragon did not move, he paused, and in a little while stole back towards it.

When he was sure that the dragon was really dead, he laughed and clapped his hands for joy, exclaiming:

"This is indeed my lucky day—now you are mine, Iseult the fair, and with you this whole wide Kingdom of Ireland."

With that he sprang on his horse and charged the dead dragon with his spear, and broke off the handle in the wound. Then, dismounting, he cut and hacked the creature with his sword: he would have cut off its head had he been able to do so, but this was beyond his powers.

Then he hunted round for the knight who had actually killed the dragon, for he felt sure that he must be lying wounded somewhere near and was determined to finish him off so that he could not contradict his lying story.

Fortunately, however, he did not find Sir Tristram, so at last he gave up the search and set out for home.

Arrived in the city, he sent out a party with a waggon to fetch home the head of the dragon, and told everyone how he had slain it. "Another man was there before me," he said, "some adventurer, doubtless. I know not who he was, but he met with an evil end for his cowardice ere I arrived: for in seeking to escape, the dragon devoured both him and his horse—the horse you may still see there, half-eaten. I have dared more for the love of a woman than ever man did before me, and tomorrow I shall claim my reward—the fair Princess Iseult to be my wife now, and the Kingdom of Ireland on her father's death."

When Iseult the fair heard of the Seneschal's deed, she came in tears to her mother: "Rather than marry him, I will slay myself!" she cried.

"It has not yet come to that," said Queen Isaud. "I do not believe that the Seneschal has indeed slain the dragon. Tonight we will discover what truly has happened."

When it was dark Iseult and her mother went secretly to the place and found the dragon dead, with the Seneschal's spear broken off in its side, and the head of the monster hacked off and carried away.

"One who had fought and slain the dragon would seek water," said Queen Isaud. And in a little while they came upon Tristram lying senseless beside the spring that gurgled into the little pool.

"Now here is a wonder," she exclaimed. "This is the minstrel Tramtris who was with us last year—but now he wears armour like a knight. But I cannot read his coat of arms, for the shield is all melted from the dragon's breath."

They had Tristram carried back to the palace, and Queen Isaud plied her arts so well that before morning he was almost recovered from the effects of the dragon's poison and able to tell them all the tale.

"Why did you come here secretly, dressed as a knight, to slay the dragon?" asked Queen Isaud.

Then Tristram told them the whole truth: that he was their sworn enemy who had slain Sir Marhault, but how he had come to win Iseult to be the bride of King Mark of Cornwall.

"No better lot could be hers," said Queen Isaud.

"Therefore, Sir Tristram of Lyonesse, if you save Iseult from the Seneschal, we will forget my brother's death and honour as our true friend and preserver the man who slew the dragon. Moreover, you shall take the Princess to be the bride of your uncle, King Mark of Cornwall, with our blessing."

When morning dawned and high noon was come, a great gathering met before the palace to see the Seneschal claim the Princess Iseult as his reward for slaying the dragon. But there was much murmuring among the crowd, for few believed that the Seneschal had indeed killed the dragon, and none wished him to marry the Princess and be their king in days to come.

When all were gathered and the King and Queen had taken their places, the Seneschal stepped forward and said:

"Your Majesty: I have slain the dragon—here is its head on a waggon to prove my words. And all these can bear witness that they saw the dragon dying from the wounds I had given it—see, here is my spear sticking in its brain—and cut off the head when life had left it."

Then rose Tristram and said: "Sire, he slew it not—I did!"

"Sire, I did slay it—and this head proves my words!" cried the Seneschal.

"My lord king," said Tristram, "since he brings the head as proof, and swears that it was lopped off by those who saw the dragon die, bid him look within the jaws. If the tongue be there, I withdraw my claim."

They opened the jaws, and found nothing there; and, as they stood amazed, Sir Tristram drew the tongue from his pouch saying:

"See now, if this be the dragon's tongue or no."

All looked, and saw that it was indeed the tongue. And

all cheered, except the Seneschal who stood there not knowing what to say nor whither to turn.

"If you doubt my word and this proof, Sir Seneschal," said Tristram, "then your course is clear: our honours are at stake—we fight to the death in single combat."

But the Seneschal was afraid to fight, and making some lame excuse, he left the place hastily amid roars of laughter, and was never seen at court again.

"Sir Tristram of Lyonesse," said King Gurman, "you have won my daughter, the fair Iseult, and with her the kingdom after my death. For no man can have any doubt that it was you who killed the dragon!"

"Noble king," said Tristram. "Fain would I wed this lovely lady, but my honour is pledged. I came hither to win her for my uncle King Mark of Cornwall—and I were shamed for ever did I take her for myself after having won her."

So Iseult set out with Brangwin her maid in Sir Tristram's ship and was wed to King Mark of Cornwall. But how she and Tristram drank the magic love-potion, not knowing what they did, and of the joy and sorrow that came to them therefrom, this tale of the slaying of the Dragon of Ireland tells not.

Sir Launcelot and the Dragon

WHEN Sir Tristram of Lyonesse came to King Arthur's court and took his place at the Round Table, only one seat remained to be filled—the Siege Perilous on which no man might sit save the best knight of all.

That year, at Whitsuntide, there came a hermit to Camelot, and when he saw the Siege Perilous, he asked who was to sit therein.

"Nay," said King Arthur and all the knights, "we know not yet who he is that shall sit there."

"But I know," said the hermit. "He is yet unborn, but ere this day next year he that shall sit in the Siege Perilous and achieve the Quest of the Holy Grail shall be born." And with these words he turned and went swiftly from their sight.

When the feast was ended Sir Launcelot rose from his seat, girded on his armour, took shield and spear in hand, and set out to seek adventures as if drawn by some hidden power.

In time he came over the Bridge of Corbyn, and there he saw the fairest tower that ever he saw, and thereunder was a fair little town full of people. And all the people, men and women at once, cried to him with one voice:

"Welcome, Sir Launcelot, the flower of knighthood! For by you we shall be helped out of our troubles."

"What mean you that you cry thus upon me?" said Sir Launcelot.

"Fair knight," they answered, "there is here within this tower a dolorous lady that has been there in pain for many seasons: for ever she boils in scalding water. But lately Sir Gawayne was here, but he might not help her, and so left her still in pain."

"Peradventure I too may leave her in her pain as Sir Gawayne did," said Sir Launcelot.

"Nay," said the people, "we know well that it is you, Sir Launcelot, that shall deliver her."

So anon they brought Launcelot into the tower. And when he came to the chamber where the lady was, the iron doors unlocked themselves and flew open before him. Forward he went, into a chamber that was as hot as any oven; and there he found as fair a lady as ever he saw, and she was as naked as a needle. For by the wicked enchantments of the witch-queen Morgana le Fay she had been imprisoned there for five years because all called her the fairest lady in the land—and there she must stay and might never be delivered until the best knight in the world took her by the hand.

Now this was Launcelot—and he led her forth and the people brought her clothes, and when she was arrayed Launcelot thought that indeed she was the fairest lady he had ever seen, except for Queen Guinevere.

Then this lady said to Launcelot: "Sir, if it please you, come with me to the chapel hard by to give thanks to God, and to complete this your quest."

So when they came to the chapel they knelt together and all the people knelt also and returned thanks for the lady's deliverance. But then they said to him:

"Sir knight, since you have delivered the lady, you must

also deliver us from the Dragon which dwells yonder in the tomb."

Then Sir Launcelot took his sword and shield, and said:

"Sirs, bring me thither, and what God gives me strength to do for you, that will I accomplish."

Then they led him to a great flat tomb, and the stone laid on it like the top of a table had these words let into it in letters of gold:

"Here shall come a Leopard of King's blood and he shall slay this Dragon. And this Leopard shall become in this country the father of a Lion, which Lion shall surpass all other Knights."

When the lid was lifted from the tomb there came out a horrible and fiendish Dragon spitting wild fire from his mouth. Then Sir Launcelot drew his sword and fought both long and fiercely with that Dragon; and at long last, with pain and difficulty Sir Launcelot slew the Dragon.

Thereafter came Pelles, King of that country and saluting him, said:

"Now, fair knight, what is your name? I require you by your knighthood, tell me."

"Sir," was the answer, "wit you well that I am Sir Launcelot of the Lake."

"And my name is King Pelles, king of this land, and descended from Joseph of Arimathea, in whose sepulchre Our Lord was laid after the Crucifixion."

Then they made much of one another, and so went up into the castle and sat down to dinner. And presently there came a Dove in through the window carrying in her mouth what seemed to be a little censor of gold, and at once the air was filled with such a sweet scent that it seemed as if all the spices in the world were there. And furthermore they found before them on the table all such meats and drinks as they could desire.

Then there came in a damsel passing fair and young, and she bore a Vessel of gold between her hands; and thereupon

the King knelt down devoutly and said a prayer—and all the company did likewise.

"In God's Name, tell me what this may mean!" said Launcelot.

"Sir," answered King Pelles, "this is the most precious thing that any man in the world may look upon; and when this thing comes to Camelot, then the Round Table will be deserted for a season. For be assured, this that you have looked upon is the Holy Grail—the Cup from which Christ and His Disciples drank at the Last Supper and which Joseph of Arimathea brought to this land."

After this Launcelot abode in the castle for many days. For King Pelles knew that the appointed time had come. For Launcelot, who had slain the Dragon, must be the father of Sir Galahad, the best knight of all who alone should achieve fully the Quest of the Holy Grail and sit in the Siege Perilous at Camelot; and Elaine, the fair lady, daughter of King Pelles was destined to be the mother of Galahad.

St. George and the Dragon

WHILE the Roman Empire still extended over most of the known world, and before the Emperor Constantine had accepted Christianity for himself and his people, there was a Christian Knight called George who was born in the Province of Cappadocia in Asia Minor.

Setting out to seek adventures, and to preach the Christian faith, George came at length to Libya in North Africa, which was then a Province of the Roman Empire bordering upon Egypt.

Now in the city of Silene dwelt a king who had one child only, a beautiful daughter called Sabra. At this time a terrible misfortune had fallen upon Silene and the country thereabout.

For by this city was a great pond or mere like a small sea wherein was a Dragon which devastated all the country. And at first the people assembled to slay him: but when they saw the terrible monster they fled.

He followed them, and when he came to the city he slew the people with his fiery breath and with the poison that streamed out of his jaws with it.

Then the people tried to keep him away by feeding him with two sheep every day. This worked well enough at first; but in time they grew short of sheep, and the Dragon began to eat the men who brought him but a single sheep instead of the two to which he had grown accustomed.

Then a law was passed that each day lots should be drawn to choose two children or young people from the city to be given to the Dragon—and on whoever the lot fell, be they the children of rich or poor, noble or peasant, there was no escape.

After many people in the city had lost their children, it chanced one day that the lot fell on Princess Sabra.

Then the King grieved sorely and said to the people:

"For love of the gods, take gold and silver and all that I have, but spare my daughter."

"Not so," they answered, "you have made and passed the law, and many of our children are now dead—you cannot change it to save your own daughter. And if you try to shield her, we will take her by force—and burn your palace over your head."

When the King saw that there was no escape, he wept, and said to Sabra:

"Alas, beloved daughter, you must be given to the Dragon. I shall not see you wedded, nor a son born to you to fill my throne."

The people gave him eight days' grace, and at the end of that time came to him saying:

"The Dragon rages for his food—and our children perish. Let your daughter be given to him as our sons and daughters have been."

Then the King arrayed Princess Sabra in wedding garments as if the day of her nuptials had come. And he kissed her and blessed her, and afterwards led her to the place where the Dragon was wont to come for his horrible meals and left her there.

As she stood weeping and shivering with fear, waiting for the Dragon, she heard the sound of horse's hooves and the clink of armour—and George of Cappadocia came riding by with his sword at his side and a spear in his hand.

"Fair lady," said he, "why do you stand here in bridal array, weeping so sorely?"

"Do not stop to ask, fair young man, but ride for your life or you will perish also," cried Sabra.

"I do not stir until you tell me of the danger and why you wait here alone to face it," he answered gravely.

Seeing that he would not go, Sabra told him of the Dragon, and of how he might be expected at any moment to come and carry her off.

Then said George of Cappadocia: "Fair lady, fear no more. For I shall save you, by the grace of Jesus Christ."

"By your gods and mine, fly swiftly, noble knight," she begged. "No one may save me, and you will only share my fate."

Even as she spoke, the reeds by the lake began to rustle, a dark smoke rose suddenly above them, and the Dragon burst into sight and came rushing hungrily towards them.

Then George leapt upon his horse, made the sign of the cross, and commending himself to God and Our Saviour set his spear in rest and charged the Dragon. So true and strong was his aim that the spear went through the monster's throat and deep into its body, and it stopped in its course and fell upon its side, grievously hurt.

George sprang from his horse, drew his sword and lashed at the Dragon, wounding it again so that it laid its head on the ground, quite overcome.

"Lady," said the knight, "take off your girdle and bind it about the head of the Dragon. Do not be afraid, it will not hurt you now."

Then Sabra did as he bade; and when she had fastened her girdle to the Dragon it followed her like a tame beast.

So she led the way to the city, the Dragon walking
beside her—and the people prepared to flee to the woods
and mountains when they saw Sabra and the Dragon
coming, crying: "Alas! Alas! We shall all be devoured
now!"

But George of Cappadocia cried in a great voice: "Do
not fear. Jesus Christ, who is the true God, has given me
the victory. Believe in Him and be baptized, and I will slay
the Dragon here and now."

Then the King and all his subjects were converted from their heathen beliefs, and George of Cappadocia baptized them one and all. Then he drew his sword and smote off the Dragon's head: and it took four carts drawn by oxen to carry its body out of the city.

Afterwards the King offered George gold and treasures. But the young knight said:

"All that you would give me, give instead to the poor. But on the spot where the Dragon fell, build a church to the glory of God—who alone gives victory."

And when the king had promised to do this, George of Cappadocia kissed him and blessed him and his people, and continued on his way.

And, after many adventures he came to Palestine where the Roman Governor Dacian cast him into prison and caused him to suffer many and terrible tortures because he would not renounce the true Faith and worship idols. And at last he was brought out for execution and his head was smitten off.

His body was buried near Joppa in the Holy Land, and when the First Crusade took Jerusalem from the Saracens a chapel to St. George was built over the tomb, which had been preserved through the years as a holy spot by the Christian Greeks who lived there.

In the tomb rested the body of St. George. But not his heart. This was brought to England by the Emperor Sigismond of Germany and given to King Henry V. And an Order of the Knights of St. George was founded at Windsor Castle, and St. George became the Patron Saint of England.

The Mummer's Play

"TWELFTH NIGHT had come and gone, and life next morning seemed a trifle flat and purposeless. But yester-eve and the Mummers were here! They had come striding into our old kitchen, powdering the red brick floor with snow from their barbaric bedizenments; and stamping and crossing, and declaiming, till all was whirl and riot and shout. . . .

"This morning, house-bound by the relentless indefatigable snow, I was feeling the reaction. Edward, on the contrary, being violently stage-struck on this his first introduction to the real Drama, was striding up and down the floor, proclaiming 'Here be I, King George the Third', in strong Berkshire accent."

So Kenneth Grahame described the coming of the Mummers in *The Golden Age,* looking back to a common recollection of country children right up to the beginning of this century.

The Mummers' Play or "St. George Play" or "Peace-Egg" dates back at least to the Middle Ages, each county having its own oral version passed down from father to son, always changing a little on the way—until it died out within living memory when country people no longer needed to make their own entertainments.

Before it was forgotten, several versions were written

87

down. The fullest was collected from a number of places by Juliana Horatia Ewing in 1884 and put together with a few lines of her own as *The Peace Egg*. Besides St. George, Sabra, the Dragon and the Doctor, it includes numerous other characters such as St. Andrew, St. David and St. Patrick, Saladin the Turkish Knight, Hector, The Valiant Slasher and the fool or "Merry Andrew". This version was revived at Bebington, Cheshire in May 1966—in which production I was lucky enough to be cast as Saladin. Our Dragon was a magnificent monster, breathing real fire, with a man in his head and front legs and a boy and a girl in his body and tail.

Mrs. Ewing's version is too long to include here, and the Berkshire version seen by Kenneth Grahame does not seem to have been written down. But from the next county, Oxfordshire, comes the following version, taken down by F. G. Lee in 1853 and published in 1874.

★

All the Mummers come in singing, and walk round the place in a circle, and then stand on one side.

Enter King Alfred and his Queen, arm in arm.

I am King Alfred, and this here is my bride.
I've a crown on my pate and a sword by my side.

Stands apart.

Enter King Cole [with a wooden leg]

I am King Cole, and I carry my stump.
Hurrah for King Charles! Down with old Noll's Rump!

Stands apart.

Enter King William [the Third]

I am King William of blessed me-mo-ry,
Who came and pulled down the high gallows-tree,
And brought us all peace and pros-peri-ty.

Stands apart.

Enter Giant Blunderbore.

I am Giant Blunderbore; fee, fi, fum!
Ready to fight you all,—so I says "Come!"

Enter Little Jack [a small boy]

And this here is my little man Jack.
A thump on his rear, and a whack on his back!

[Strikes him twice]

I'll fight King Alfred, I'll fight King Cole,
I'm ready to fight any mortal soul!
So here I, Blunderbore, takes my stand,
With this little devil, Jack, at my right hand,
Ready to fight for mortal life. Fee, fi, fum.

[The Giant and Little Jack stand apart]

Enter St. George.

I am St. George of Merry Eng-land.
Bring in our morres-men, bring in our band.

Morres-men come in and dance to a tune from fife and drum. The dance ended, St. George continues:

These are our tricks, ho! men, ho!
These are our sticks,—whack men so!

He strikes the Dragon, who roars and comes forward.

The Dragon speaks:

I am the Dragon,—here are my jaws!
I am the Dragon,—here are my claws!
Meat, meat, meat for to eat!
Stand on my head, stand on my feet!

Turns a somersault and stands aside.

All sing, several times repeated:

Ho! Ho! Ho!
Whack men so!

The drum and fife sound. They all fight, and after general disorder, fall down.

Enter old Dr. Ball.

I am the Doctor, and I cure all ills,
Only gulp my potions, and swallow my pills;
I can cure the itch, the stitch, the pox, the palsy, and the
     gout,
All pains within and all pains without.
Up from the floor, Giant Blunderbore!
Get up, King! get up Bride!
Get up, Fool, and stand aside!

He gives them each a pill, and they rise at once.

Get up, King Cole, and tell the gentle folks all
There never was a doctor like Mr. Doctor Ball.
Get up, St. George, old England's knight!
You have wounded the Dragon and finished the fight.

All stand aside but the Dragon, who lies in convulsions on the floor.

Now kill the Dragon and poison old Nick;
At Yule-tyde both o' ye, cut your stick!

The Doctor forces a large pill down the Dragon's throat, who thereupon roars, and dies in convulsions. Then enter Father Christmas:

I am Father Christmas! Hold, men, hold!

[Addressing the audience]

Be there loaf in your locker and sheep in your fold,
A fire on the hearth, and good luck for your lot,
Money in your pocket, and a pudding in the pot!

He sings

Hold, men, hold!
Put up your sticks;
End all your tricks;
Hold, men, hold!

Chorus (all sing, while going round with a hat for gifts)

Hold, men, hold!
We are very cold,

Inside and outside,
We are very cold.
If you don't give us silver,
Then give us gold
From the money in your pockets!

God Almighty bless your hearth and fold,
Shut out the wolf, and keep out the cold!
You gev' us silver, keep you the gold,
For 'tis in your pocket.—Hold, men, hold!

They all go out, singing.

★

"The room was quieter now, for Edward had got the
Dragon down, and was boring holes in him with a purring
sound. . . ."

" 'Now I want a live Dragon,' he announced. 'You've
got to be my Dragon!'

" 'Leave me go, will you?' squealed Harold, struggling
stoutly. 'I'm playing at something else. How can I be a
dragon and belong to all the clubs?'

" 'But wouldn't you like to be a nice scaly Dragon, all
green,' said Edward, trying persuasion, 'with a curly tail
and red eyes, and breathing real smoke and fire?' "

"Harold wavered an instant: Pall-Mall was still strong on
him. The next he was grovelling on the floor. No saurian
ever swung a tail so scaly and so curly as his. Clubland was
a thousand years away. With horrific pants he emitted
smokiest smoke and fiercest fire.

" 'Now I want a Princess,' cried Edward, clutching
Charlotte ecstatically; 'and *you* can be the Doctor, and heal
me from the Dragon's deadly wound . . .' "

Sir John Maundeville's Dragon

Although the account of Sir John Maundeville's travels to the Holy Land in the middle of the Fourteenth Century was, in fact, a work of fiction composed by Jean d'Outremeuse (1338–1400) Maundeville seems to have been a real person. And certainly his "Travels" were accepted as a true account of the strange lands in the east that pilgrims might visit on their way to Jerusalem.

. . . And then men pass through the isles of Cophos and Lango (Cos) of which isles Ipocras (Hippocrates) was lord. And some say that in the isle of Lango is Ipocras's daughter in the form of a Dragon, which is a hundred foot long as men say, for I have not seen it. And they of the isles call her the lady of the country, and she lieth in an old castle and showeth herself thrice in the year, and she doth no man any harm.

And she is thus changed from a damsel to a dragon by the goddess that men call Diana; and men say that she shall dwell so unto the time that a knight come that is so daring as to go to her and kiss her mouth, and then she shall turn again into her own shape, and be a woman, and after that she shall not live long. And it is not long since a Knight of Rhodes that was hardy and valiant said that he would kiss her, and when the Dragon began to lift up her head against him, and he saw it was so hideous, he fled away, and the Dragon in her anger seized the Knight, carried him to the top of a cliff and cast him thence into the sea so that he perished.

93

Also a young man that knew not of the Dragon, left his ship and went through the isle till he came to the castle, and came into the cave, and went deep into it until he found a chamber where he saw a damsel that combed her hair and looked at herself in a mirror. She had much treasure all round her, and he thought she must be some common woman who dwelt there to entertain wandering men.

So he bowed to her, and the damsel saw the reflection of him in her mirror, and she turned towards him and asked what he wanted. He said that he would like her to be his sweetheart, and she asked him if he were a knight, and he said, "No".

Then she said that she could not be his sweetheart, but she bade him go back to his companions and be dubbed a knight—then come again next day and she would come out of the cave, and then he should kiss her on the mouth. And she bade him have no fear, for she would do him no harm although she would then seem to him hideous.

"For," said she, "I am under an enchantment, and in truth I am really as you see me now. And if you kiss me, you shall have all this treasure and be my lord, and the lord of all these isles."

Then he departed from her and went to his companions in the ship, and they dubbed him knight.

And he came back next morning to kiss the damsel. But when he saw her come out of the cave in the form of a Dragon, he was so terrified that he fled to the ship. She followed him; and when she saw that he would not come back she began to cry like a creature in deep sorrow, and returned weeping to her cave.

Soon after this the knight died, and since then no knight has seen her and lived for long. But when a knight comes that is brave enough to kiss her, he shall not die, but he shall turn that damsel into her true shape and shall be lord of that country.

And from thence men go to the isle of Rhodes. . . .

The Dragons of Rhodes, Lucerne
and Somerset

IT is odd that Sir John Maundeville did not mention the Dragon who lived in the island of Rhodes and met its death in 1345, only a few years before his Travels to the Holy Land.

The Dragon of Rhodes dwelt in a cave on Mount St. Stephen just above the city of Rhodes itself. It devoured sheep, cattle, men, anything living that it could seize— and anyone who tried to kill it met an unpleasant end, poisoned by its breath before being eaten.

It was so dangerous, in fact, that the Grand Master of the Knights of Rhodes forbade any members of the Order to go against it. Fortunately for the City of the Knights, however, one of his followers, a young Gascon Knight called Deodatus de Gozon disobeyed his commands and set himself to exterminate the Dragon.

This he did by retiring into the centre of the island with his men and two fierce English bulldogs, and training them carefully with the aid of an imitation Dragon which he made of wires and parchment stuffed with tow.

When all was ready, he set out for Mount St. Stephen with his trusty followers. On reaching the cave, the Knight entered it bravely and began to yell lustily in order to wake the Dragon and annoy it. As soon as he succeeded in doing this, he rushed out of the cave, leapt upon his charger, and made ready to receive the enemy.

Presently out came the Dragon hissing with fury and clattering its wings. De Gozon hurled his spear, but it broke to pieces on the Dragon's scales, and he would have fallen an easy victim had not the dogs rushed in and seized the creature on either side.

The Dragon reared up on end and, like a bear, tried to hug its enemies to death. But this exposed the under surface of its neck where the scales were thin, and the Knight was able to thrust his sword deep into the monster's throat so that the blood gushed out. The Dragon tottered and fell; but in its fall it crushed De Gozon to the ground, and he would have died from the weight of the creature and its venomous blood, had not his men rushed forward and dragged him out just in time.

De Gozon lived to become Grand Master of the Knights himself, and the remains of the Dragon were preserved for nearly four centuries and shown to all visitors to the island. The creature was described in the middle of the seventeenth century by Athanasius Kircher in his book on caves and cave dwellers, *Mundus Subterraneus* (1665) who seems to be quoting from the annals of the Knights of Rhodes themselves:

"This monster is described as of the bulk of a horse or ox, with a long neck and serpent's head—tipped with mule's ears—the mouth widely gaping and furnished with sharp teeth, eyes sparkling as though they flashed fire, four feet provided with claws like a bear, and a tail like a crocodile, the whole body being coated with hard scales. It had two wings, blue above, but blood-coloured and yellow underneath; it was swifter than a horse, progressing partly by flight and partly by running."

While collecting material for his book on caves and their inhabitants, Kircher visited Lucerne in Switzerland and saw in the Church of St. Leodegaris the monument to Victor of Lucerne who had left all his goods to the Church when he died shortly after an amazing experience with two dragons.

Victor, so Kircher was told, was a cooper or barrel-maker, who was wandering one day on nearby Mount Pilatus (already well known as a favourite dwelling-place for dragons). He was seeking for wood out of which to make casks, and lost his way in the forest high up on the mountain side. All day he wandered there until, as darkness was falling he began looking for some sheltered place in which to spend the night. But, in the failing light, he fell into a deep chasm which was hidden by a fringe of bushes and long grass.

Fortunately Victor landed in soft mud at the bottom of the chasm, and did not break any bones, though the shock of the fall knocked him out. When he recovered, he began to grope about, and soon realized that he was at the bottom of a great cleft in the rock with sheer sides up which it was quite impossible to climb.

In the morning he continued his search in such light as filtered down to him, but all in vain. He found, however, several caves in the side of the cleft and began to explore them one by one in the hope of finding that one led out on to the mountain side.

Suddenly he shrank back in terror, thinking his last moment had come. For out of the biggest of the caves came two huge winged dragons. They were fearsome beasts indeed, though they did not breath fire or poison; but they did not seem to be in the least savage. On the contrary, they showed great curiosity as to their new companion, and rubbed their scaley sides against Victor in the friendliest fashion, making a loud purring sound as if they were giant cats.

For six months Victor lived with the dragons in their cave. Somehow he managed to exist with little or no food, for there was plenty of water dripping down the rocks. But without the dragons he would certainly have died in the bitter cold at night had he not been able to shelter among their coils in the cave.

When spring came the dragons became restless: and one day the larger of the two suddenly spread his wings and flew up out of the chasm. As the second was about to follow, Victor seized his only opportunity of escape, clasped the dragon by the tail, and was carried safely up on to the mountain side.

He found his way back to Lucerne in safety, and told his wonderful tale. Unfortunately, however, his return to ordinary diet proved fatal, and he died shortly afterwards —leaving all his goods to the Church.

Stories of dragons attached firmly to certain places lead on from legend to fairytale. The first two stories in the next section of this book form a good link between the two—and to introduce them here is a dragon tale from Somerset:

"There came a great dragon to Shervage Wood. It had no wings, and was more like a mighty worm. But such a worm! It was as long and fat as the trunks of three great oak-trees laid end to end! He swallowed sheep and ponies, and when shepherds or gipsies went too near—he swallowed them too. After a while no one cared to go anywhere near Shervage Wood: though the worts were ripening there, no one could go and pick them.

"There was an old woman who got her living from the

worts, and she did not dare to go gathering them. So one day when a stranger came along, a wood-cutter from Stogumber, she told him there were good faggots to be cut up in Shervage Wood. She gave the wood-cutter some cider and bread-and-cheese; but she did not say anything about the dragon.

"It was a steep hill up to the Wood, and when he got there the wood-cutter sat down to rest on a fallen log, and took a deep draught of cider. The log began to wriggle about very strangely.

"'You keep still!' shouted the wood-cutter, and he struck the log with his axe. It went through it like butter; blood ran out. He had cut the dragon in half!

"One half of the dragon rushed down the hill to Bilbrook and the other half to Kingston St. Mary. And since they set out in opposite directions they never met, and so the Dragon of Shervage Wood could not join together again—and that was the end of it!"

PART THREE

Dragons of Folklore

The Laidly Worm

Retold by JOSEPH JACOBS

IN Bamborough Castle once lived a king who had a fair
wife and two children, a son named Childe Wynd and
a daughter named Margaret. Childe Wynd went forth
to seek his fortune, and soon after he had gone the queen his
mother died. The king mourned her long and faithfully,
but one day while he was hunting he came across a lady
of great beauty, and became so much in love with her that
he determined to marry her. So he sent word home that
he was going to bring a new queen to Bamborough
Castle.

Princess Margaret was not very glad to hear of her
mother's place being taken, but she did not repine but did
her father's bidding, and at the appointed day came down
to the castle gate with the keys all ready to hand over to
her step-mother. Soon the procession drew near, and the
new queen came towards Princess Margaret who bowed
low and handed her the keys of the castle. She stood there
with blushing cheeks and eye on ground, and said: "O
welcome, father dear, to your halls and bowers, and welcome to you my new mother, for all that's here is yours,"
and again she offered the keys. One of the king's knights
who had escorted the new queen, cried out in admiration:
"Surely this northern Princess is the loveliest of her kind."
At that the new queen flushed up and cried out: "At least

your courtesy might have excepted me," and then she
muttered below her breath: "I'll soon put an end to her
beauty."

That same night the queen, who was a noted witch, stole
down to a lonely dungeon wherein she did her magic and
with spells three times three, and with passes nine times
nine she cast Princess Margaret under her spell. And this
was her spell:

> I weird ye to be a Laidly Worm,
>   And borrowed shall ye never be,
> Until Childe Wynd, the King's own son
>   Come to the Heugh and thrice kiss thee;
> Until the world comes to an end,
>   Borrowed shall ye never be.

So Lady Margaret went to bed a beauteous maiden, and
rose up a Laidly Worm. And when her maidens came in to
dress her in the morning they found coiled up on the bed
a dreadful dragon, which uncoiled itself and came towards
them. But they ran away shrieking, and the Laidly Worm
crawled and crept, and crept and crawled till it reached the
Heugh or rock of the Spindlestone, round which it coiled
itself, and lay there basking with its terrible snout in the
air.

Soon the country round about had reason to know of
the Laidly Worm of Spindlestone Heugh. For hunger drove
the monster out from its cave and it used to devour everything it could come across. So at last they went to a mighty
warlock and asked him what they should do. Then he
consulted his works and his familiar, and told them: "The
Laidly Worm is really the Princess Margaret and it is
hunger that drives her forth to do such deeds. Put aside for

her seven kine, and each day as the sun goes down, carry every drop of milk they yield to the stone trough at the foot of the Heugh, and the Laidly Worm will trouble the country no longer. But if ye would that she be borrowed to her natural shape, and that she who bespelled her be rightly punished, send over the seas for her brother, Childe Wynd."

All was done as the warlock advised, the Laidly Worm lived on the milk of the seven kine, and the country was troubled no longer. But when Childe Wynd heard the news, he swore a mighty oath to rescue his sister and revenge her on her cruel stepmother. And three-and-thirty of his men took the oath with him. Then they set to work and built a long ship, and its keel they made of the rowan tree. And when all was ready, they out with their oars and pulled sheer for Bamborough Keep.

But as they got near the keep, the stepmother felt by her magic power that something was being wrought against her, so she summoned her familiar imps and said: "Childe Wynd is coming over the seas; he must never land. Raise storms, or bore the hull, but nohow must he touch shore." Then the imps went forth to meet Childe Wynd's ship, but when they got near, they found they had no power over the ship, for its keel was made of the rowan tree. So back they came to the queen witch, who knew not what to do. She ordered her men-at-arms to resist Childe Wynd if he should land near them, and by her spells she caused the Laidly Worm to wait by the entrance of the harbour.

As the ship came near, the Worm unfolded its coils, and dipping into the sea, caught hold of the ship of Childe Wynd, and banged it off the shore. Three times Childe Wynd urged his men on to row bravely and strong, but each time the Laidly Worm kept it off the shore. Then

Childe Wynd ordered the ship to be put about, and the witch-queen thought he had given up the attempt. But instead of that, he only rounded the next point and landed safe and sound in Budle Creek, and then, with sword drawn and bow bent, rushed up followed by his men, to fight the terrible Worm that had kept him from landing.

But the moment Childe Wynd had landed, the witch-queen's power over the Laidly Worm had gone, and she went back to her bower all alone, not an imp, nor a man-at-arms to help her, for she knew her hour was come. So when Childe Wynd came rushing up to the Laidly Worm it made no attempt to stop him or hurt him, but just as he was going to raise his sword to slay it, the voice of his own sister Margaret came from its jaws saying:

> "O, quit your sword, unbend your bow,
>   And give me kisses three;
> For though I am a poisonous worm,
>   No harm I'll do to thee."

Childe Wynd stayed his hand, but he did not know what to think if some witchery were not in it. Then said the Laidly Worm again:

"O, quit your sword, unbend your bow,
　And give me kisses three,
If I'm not won ere set of sun,
　Won never shall I be."

Then Childe Wynd went up to the Laidly Worm and kissed it once; but no change came over it. Then Childe Wynd kissed it once more; but yet no change came over it. For a third time he kissed the loathsome thing, and with a hiss and a roar the Laidly Worm reared back and before Childe Wynd stood his sister Margaret. He wrapped his cloak about her, and then went up to the castle with her. When he reached the keep, he went off to the witch queen's bower, and when he saw her, he touched her with a twig of a rowan tree. No sooner had he touched her than she

shrivelled up and shrivelled up, till she became a huge ugly toad, with bold staring eyes and a horrible hiss. She croaked and she hissed, and then hopped away down the castle steps, and Childe Wynd took his father's place as king, and they all lived happy afterwards.

But to this day, the loathsome toad is seen at times, haunting the neighbourhood of Bamborough Keep, and the wicked witch-queen is a Laidly Toad.

The Lambton Worm

Retold by JOSEPH JACOBS

A wild young fellow was the heir of Lambton, the fine estate and hall by the side of the swift-flowing Wear. Not a Mass would he hear in Brugeford Chapel of a Sunday, but a-fishing he would go. And if he did not haul in anything, his curses could be heard by the folk as they went by to Brugeford.

Well, one Sunday morning he was fishing as usual, and not a salmon had risen to him, his basket was bare of roach or dace. And the worse his luck, the worse grew his language, till the passers-by were horrified at his words as they went to listen to the Mass-priest.

At last young Lambton felt a mighty tug at his line. "At last," quoth he, "a bite worth having!" and he pulled and he pulled, till what should appear above the water but a head like an eft's, with nine holes on each side of its mouth. But still he pulled till he had got the thing to land, when it turned out to be a Worm of hideous shape. If he had cursed before, his curses were enough to raise the hair on your head.

"What ails thee, my son?" said a voice by his side, "and what hast thou caught, that thou shouldst stain the Lord's Day with such foul language?"

Looking round, young Lambton saw a strange old man standing by him.

"Why, truly," he said, "I think I have caught the devil himself. Look you and see if you know him."

But the stranger shook his head, and said, "It bodes no good to thee or thine to bring such a monster to shore. Yet cast him not back into the Wear; thou hast caught him, and thou must keep him," and with that away he turned, and was seen no more.

The young heir of Lambton took up the gruesome thing, and, taking it off his hook, cast it into a well close by, and ever since that day that well has gone by the name of the Worm Well.

For some time nothing more was seen or heard of the Worm, till one day it had outgrown the size of the well, and came forth full-grown. So it came forth from the well and betook itself to the Wear. And all day long it would lie coiled round a rock in the middle of the stream, while at night it came forth from the river and harried the countryside. It sucked the cows' milk, devoured the lambs, worried the cattle, and frightened all the women and girls of the district, and then it would retire for the rest of the night to the hill, still called the Worm Hill, on the north side of the Wear, about a mile and a half from Lambton Hall.

This terrible visitation brought young Lambton, of Lambton Hall, to his senses. He took upon himself the vows of the Cross, and departed for the Holy Land, in the hope that the scourge he had brought upon his district would disappear. But the grisly Worm took no heed, except that it crossed the river and came right up to Lambton Hall itself where the old lord lived on all alone, his only son having gone to the Holy Land. What to do? The Worm was coming closer and closer to the Hall; women were shrieking, men were gathering weapons, dogs were barking and horses neighing with terror. At last the steward called out to the dairy maids, "Bring all your milk hither," and when they did so, and had brought all the milk that the nine kye of the byre had yielded, he poured it all into the long stone trough in front of the Hall.

The Worm drew nearer and nearer, till at last it came up to the trough. But when it sniffed the milk, it turned aside to the trough and swallowed all the milk up, and then slowly turned round and crossed the river Wear, and coiled its bulk three times round the Worm Hill for the night.

Henceforth the Worm would cross the river every day, and woe betide the Hall if the trough contained the milk of less than nine kye. The Worm would hiss, and would rave, and lash its tail round the trees of the park, and in its fury it would uproot the stoutest oaks and the loftiest firs. So it went on for seven years. Many tried to destroy the Worm, but all had failed, and many a knight had lost his life in fighting with the monster, which slowly crushed the life out of all that came near it.

At last the Childe of Lambton came home to his father's Hall, after seven long years spent in meditation and repentance on holy soil. Sad and desolate he found his folk; the lands untilled, the farms deserted, half the trees of the park uprooted, for none would stay to tend the nine kye that the monster needed for his food each day.

The Childe sought his father, and begged his forgiveness for the curse he had brought on the Hall.

"Thy sin is pardoned," said his father; "but go thou to the Wise Woman of Brugeford, and find if aught can free us from this monster."

To the Wise Woman went the Childe, and asked her advice.

"'Tis thy fault, O Childe, for which we suffer," she said: "be it thine to release us."

"I would give my life," said the Childe.

"Mayhap thou wilt do so," said she. "But hear me, and mark me well. Thou, and thou alone, canst kill the Worm. But, to this end, thou go to the smithy and have thy armour studded with spear-heads. Then go to the Worm's Rock in the Wear, and station thyself there. Then, when the Worm comes to the Rock at dawn of day, try thy prowess on him, and God gi'e thee a good deliverance."

"And this I will do," said Childe Lambton.

"But one thing more," said the Wise Woman, going back to her cell. "If thou slay the Worm, swear that thou wilt put to death the first thing that meets thee as thou crossest again the threshold of Lambton Hall. Do this, and all will be well with thee and thine. Fulfil not thy vow, and none of the Lambtons, for generations three times three, shall die in his bed. Swear, and fail not."

The Childe swore as the Wise Woman bid, and went his way to the smithy. There he had his armour studded with spear-heads all over. Then he passed his vigils in Brugeford Chapel, and at dawn of day took his post on the Worm's Rock in the River Wear.

As dawn broke, the Worm uncoiled its snaky twine from around the hill, and came to its rock in the river. When it perceived the Childe waiting for it, it lashed the waters in its fury and wound its coils round the Childe, and then attempted to crush him to death. But the more it pressed, the deeper dug the spear-heads into its sides. Still it pressed and pressed, till all the water around was crimsoned with its blood. Then the Worm unwound itself, and left the Childe free to use his sword. He raised it, brought it down, and cut the Worm in two. One half fell into the

river, and was carried swiftly away. Once more the head
and the remainder of the body encircled the Childe, but
with less force, and the spear-heads did their work. At last
the Worm uncoiled itself, snorted its last foam of blood
and fire, and rolled dying into the river, and was never
seen more.

The Childe of Lambton swam ashore, and, raising his
bugle to his lips, sounded its note thrice. This was the
signal to the Hall, where the servants and the old lord had
shut themselves in to pray for the Childe's success. When
the third sound of the bugle was heard, they were to
release Boris, the Childe's favourite hound. But such was
their joy at learning of the Childe's safety and the Worm's
defeat, that they forgot orders, and when the Childe
reached the threshold of the Hall his old father rushed out
to meet him, and would have clasped him to his breast.

"The vow! The vow!" called out the Childe of Lambton
and blew still another blast upon his horn. This time the
servants remembered, and released Boris, who came
bounding to his young master. The Childe raised his
shining sword, and severed the head of his faithful hound.

But the vow was broken, and for nine generations of
men none of the Lambtons died in his bed. The last of the
Lambtons died in his carriage as he was crossing Brugeford
Bridge, one hundred and thirty years ago.

The Little Bull-Calf

Retold by JOSEPH JACOBS

CENTURIES of years ago, when almost all this part of the country was wilderness, there was a little boy, who lived in a poor bit of property and his father gave him a little bull-calf, and with it he gave him everything he wanted for it.

But soon after his father died, and his mother got married again to a man that turned out to be a very vicious stepfather, who couldn't abide the little boy. So at last the stepfather said: "If you bring that bull-calf into this house, I'll kill it." What a villain he was, wasn't he?

Now this little boy used to go out and feed his bull-calf every day with barley bread, and when he did so this time, an old man came up to him—we can guess who that was, eh?—and said to him: "You and your bull-calf had better go away and seek your fortune."

So he went on and he went on and he went on, as far as I could tell you till tomorrow night, and he went up to a farmhouse and begged a crust of bread, and when he got back he broke it in two and gave half of it to the bull-calf. And he went to another house and begged a bit of cheese crud, and when he went back he wanted to give half of it to the bull-calf. "No," says the bull-calf, "I'm going across the field, into the wild-wood wilderness country, where there'll be tigers, leopards, wolves, monkeys, and a fiery

dragon, and I'll kill them all except the fiery dragon, and
he'll kill me."

The little boy did cry, and said: "Oh no, my little
bull-calf; I hope he won't kill you."

"Yes, he will," said the little bull-calf, "so you climb up
that tree, so that no one can come nigh you but the monkeys, and if they come the cheese crud will save you. And
when I'm killed, the dragon will go away for a bit, then
you must come down the tree and skin me, and take out
my bladder and blow it out, and it will kill everything you
hit with it. So when the fiery dragon comes back, you hit
it with my bladder and cut its tongue out."

(We know there were fiery dragons in those days, like
George and his Dragon in the Bible; but there! it's not the
same world nowadays. The world is turned topsy-turvy
since then, like as if you'd turned it over with a spade!)

Of course he did all the little bull-calf told him. He

climbcd up the tree, and the monkeys climbed up the tree after him. But he held the cheese crud in his hand, and said: "I'll squeeze your heart like the flint-stone." So the monkey cocked his eye as much as to say: "If you can squeeze a flint-stone to make the juice come out of it, you can squeeze me." But he didn't say anything, for a monkey's cunning, but down he went. And all the while the little bull-calf was fighting all the wild beasts on the ground, and the little lad was clapping his hands up the tree, and calling out: "Go in, my little bull-calf! Well fought, little bull-calf!" And he mastered everything except the fiery dragon, but the fiery dragon killed the little bull-calf.

But the lad waited and waited till he saw the dragon go away, then he came down and skinned the little bull-calf, and took out its bladder and went after the dragon. And as he went on, what should he see but a king's daughter, staked down by the hair of her head, for she had been put there for the dragon to destroy her.

So he went up and untied her hair, but she said: "My time has come, for the dragon to destroy me; go away, you can do no good." But he said: "No! I can master it, and I won't go;" and for all her begging and praying he would stop.

And soon he heard it coming, roaring and raging from afar off, and at last it came near, spitting fire and with a tongue like a great spear, and you could hear it roaring for miles, and it was making for the place where the king's daughter was staked down. But when it came up to them, the lad just hit it on the head with the bladder and the dragon fell down dead, but before it died, it bit off the little boy's forefinger.

Then the lad cut out the dragon's tongue and said to the

king's daughter: "I've done all I can, I must leave you."
And sorry she was he had to go, and before he went she
tied a diamond ring in his hair, and said goodbye to him.

By-and-by, who should come along but the old king,
lamenting and weeping, and expecting to see nothing of
his daughter but the prints of the place where she had been.
But he was surprised to find her there alive and safe, and he
said: "How came you to be saved?" So she told him how
she had been saved, and he took her home to his castle
again.

Well, he put it into all the papers to find out who saved
his daughter, and who had the dragon's tongue and the
princess's diamond ring, and was without his forefinger.
Whoever could show these signs should marry his daughter
and have his kingdom after his death. Well, any number of
gentlemen came from all parts of England, with fore-
fingers cut off, and with diamond rings and all kinds of
tongues, wild beasts' tongues and foreign tongues. But
they couldn't show any dragons' tongues, so they were
turned away.

At last the little boy turned up, looking very ragged and
desolated like, and the king's daughter cast her eye on him,
till her father grew very angry and ordered them to turn
the little beggar boy away. "Father," says she; "I know
something of that boy."

Well, still the fine gentlemen came, bringing up their
dragons' tongues that weren't dragons' tongues, and at
last the little boy came up, dressed a little better. So the old
king says: "I see you've got an eye on that boy. If it has to
be him it must be him." But all the others were fit to kill
him, and cried out: "Pooh, pooh, turn that boy out, it
can't be him." But the king said: "Now my boy, let's see
what you have to show." Well, he showed the diamond

ring with her name on it, and the fiery dragon's tongue. How the others were thunderstruck when he showed his proofs! But the king told him: "You shall have my daughter and my estate."

So he married the princess, and afterwards got the king's estate. Then his stepfather came and wanted to own him, but the young king didn't know such a man.

The Dragon and his Grandmother

Translated from Grimm by MAY SELLAR

THERE was once a great war, and the King had a great many soldiers, but he could give them so little pay that they could not live upon it. Then three of them took counsel together and determined to desert.

One of them said to the others, "If we are caught we shall be hanged on the gallows; how shall we set about it?" The other said, "Do you see that large cornfield there? If we were to hide ourselves in that, no one could find us. The army cannot come into it, and tomorrow it is to march on."

They crept into the corn, but the army did not march on, but remained encamped close around them. They sat for two days and two nights in the corn, and grew so hungry that they nearly died; but if they were to venture out, it was certain death.

They said at last, "What use was it our deserting? We must perish here miserably."

Whilst they were speaking a fiery Dragon came flying through the air. It hovered near them, and asked why they were hidden there. They answered, "We are three soldiers, and have deserted because our pay was so small. Now if we remain here we shall die of hunger, and if we move out we shall be strung up on the gallows."

"If you will serve me for seven years," said the Dragon,

"I will lead you through the midst of the army so that no one shall catch you." "We have no choice, and must take your offer," said they. Then the Dragon seized them in his claws, took them through the air over the army, and set them down on the earth a long way from it.

He gave them a little whip, saying, "Whip and slash with this, and as much money as you want will jump up before you. You can then live as great lords, keep horses, and drive about in carriages. But after seven years you are mine." Then he put a book before them, which he made all three of them sign. "I will then give you a riddle," he said; "if you guess it, you shall be free and out of my power." The dragon then flew away, and they journeyed on with their little whip. They had as much money as they wanted, wore grand clothes, and made their way into the world. Wherever they went they lived in merry-making and splendour, drove about with horses and carriages, ate and drank, but did nothing wrong.

The time passed quickly away, and when the seven years were nearly ended two of them grew terribly anxious and frightened, but the third made light of it, saying, "Don't be afraid, brothers, I wasn't born yesterday: I will guess the riddle."

They went into a field, sat down, and the two pulled long faces. An old woman passed by, and asked them why they were so sad. "Alas! what have you to do with it? You cannot help us." "Who knows?" she answered. "Only confide your trouble in me."

Then they told her that they had become the servants of the Dragon for seven long years, and how he had given them money as plentifully as blackberries; but as they had signed their names they were his, unless when the seven years had passed they could guess a riddle. The old woman said, "If you would help yourselves, one of you must go into the wood, and there he will come upon a tumble-down building of rocks which looks like a little house. He must go in, and there he will find help."

The two melancholy ones thought, "That won't save us!" and they remained where they were. But the third and merry one jumped up and went into the wood till he found the rock hut. In the hut sat a very old woman, who was the Dragon's grandmother. She asked him how he came, and what was his business there. He told her all that happened, and because she was pleased with him she took compassion on him, and said she would help him.

She lifted up a large stone which lay over the cellar, saying, "Hide yourself there; you can hear all that is spoken in this room. Only sit still and don't stir. When the Dragon comes, I will ask him what the riddle is, for he tells me everything; then listen carefully what he answers."

At midnight the Dragon flew in, and asked for his supper. His grandmother laid the table, and brought out food and drink till he was satisfied, and they ate and drank together. Then in the course of the conversation she asked him what he had done in the day, and how many souls he had conquered.

"I haven't had much luck today," he said, "but I have a tight hold on three soldiers."

"Indeed! three soldiers!" said she. "Who cannot escape you?"

"They are mine," answered the Dragon scornfully, "for I shall only give them one riddle which they will never be able to guess."

"What sort of a riddle is it?" she asked.

"I will tell you this. In the North Sea lies a dead sea-cat —that shall be their roast meat; and the rib of a whale—

that shall be their silver spoon; and the hollow foot of a dead horse—that shall be their wineglass."

When the Dragon had gone to bed, his old grandmother pulled up the stone and let out the soldier.

"Did you pay attention to everything?"

"Yes," he replied, "I know enough, and can help myself splendidly." Then he went by another way through the window secretly, and in all haste back to his comrades. He told them how the Dragon had been outwitted by his grandmother, and how he had heard from his own lips the answer to the riddle.

Then they were all delighted and in high spirits, took out their whip and cracked so much money that it came jumping up from the ground. When the seven years had quite gone, the Dragon came with his book, and, pointing at the signatures, said, "I will take you underground with me; you shall have a meal there. If you can tell me what you will get for your roast meat, you shall be free, and shall also keep the whip."

Then said the first soldier, "In the North Sea lies a dead sea-cat; that shall be the roast meat."

The Dragon was much annoyed, and hummed and hawed a good deal, and asked the second, "But what shall be your spoon?"

"The rib of a whale shall be our silver spoon."

The Dragon made a face, and growled again three times, "Hum, hum, hum," and said to the third, "Do you know what your wine-glass shall be?"

"An old horse's hoof shall be our wineglass."

Then the Dragon flew away with a loud shriek, and had no more power over them. But the three soldiers took the little whip, whipped as much money as they wanted, and lived happily to their lives' end.

The Dragon of the North

VERY long ago there lived a terrible Dragon who came out of the North and laid waste whole countries, devouring both men and beasts; and this monster was so destructive that people feared that unless help came no living creature would be left on the face of the earth.

This Dragon had a body like an ox, legs like a frog—two short forelegs, and two longer ones behind—and a tail like a serpent sixty feet long. When it moved it jumped like a frog, and with every spring it covered half a mile of ground. It was accustomed to remain in one place for several years at a time, and not to move far until the whole neighbourhood was eaten up.

Nothing could hurt it because its whole body was covered with scales which were harder than stone or metal: its two eyes blazed with fire both day and night, and they had the power of bewitching anyone who looked at them, so that he would rush of his own accord into the Dragon's huge jaws.

Every time the Dragon settled in a new place, the king of that country would offer his daughter in marriage and rich rewards of gold and jewels to whoever could kill the Dragon. Many tried to do so, but all of them perished in the attempt; and once when a forest in which the Dragon slept was set on fire all round him, he took no harm at all—

but the country was short of timber for years to come.

The time came when a young Prince with his fortune to make fell in love with the Princess of the country in which the Dragon happened to be—and determined to win her. But he was a wise young man, who took the trouble first of all to consult the sages and magicians of that and all the neighbouring countries, until he found one who said:

"No one can overcome the Dragon by his own skill or bravery; and no magician in this part of the world has charms strong enough to prevail against it. But if you travel east you may find King Solomon's Ring—and if then you can read the secret writing engraved on it, then surely you will be able to conquer this or any dragon."

So the Prince set out, and after many adventures came to an enchanter in an eastern land who was able to help him. This he did by brewing a magic potion which gave the Prince the power to understand all that the birds were saying.

"The birds fly everywhere," said the enchanter, "and they, if any living creature does, will know where King Solomon's Ring lies hidden. Go on your way, and listen, ever listen to the talk of the birds. It may be that one day you will hear what you wish to know."

And at last the time arrived when the enchanter's words came true.

The Prince was lying half-asleep one evening under a tree, when he heard two birds chattering to one another up in the branches over his head.

"Look at that silly young man," said one bird. "He's trying to find King Solomon's Ring! *He'll* never succeed!"

"He'd need to find the Witch Maiden first," said the other bird. "If she has not got the Ring herself, she knows where it lies hidden."

"True," answered the first bird. "But she never stays in one place for long. He might just as well try to catch the wind!"

"She'll be at the pool in the forest at full moon," said the other bird. "She comes there every month to wash her face in the magic water so that it may never grow old and wrinkled."

"I've never seen her," said the second bird. "Show me where the pool is, and we'll sit up in a tree and watch her."

The Prince pretended that he had not understood a word of what the birds had been talking about. But when they flew off, he followed them as if by chance and sat down again under a tree by the pool to which they led him.

"Here's that silly young man again," said one bird. "I expect the Witch Maiden will catch him."

"He'll never have the sense to realize that he's perfectly safe from her if he doesn't let her have a single drop of his blood," said the other.

Presently the Witch Maiden came, more beautiful than the moonlight, and bathed her face nine times in the magic pool.

Then she saw the Prince, greeted him kindly, and took him with her to her palace where she entertained him for many days and at length tried to persuade him to become her husband, sealing the compact with three drops of his blood.

But he put her off from day to day, and as she grew more and more anxious to win him, she gave away more and more of her secrets, until at last she took King Solomon's Ring out of a golden casket and told him about it.

"No mortal knows all the power of this Ring, for none

can read the secret words carved on it. But I have discovered as much as may be known. If I put it on the little
finger of my left hand, than I can fly like a bird. If I put it
on the third finger of my left hand, I become invisible. If
I put it on the middle finger of that hand neither fire nor
water nor any sharp weapon can hurt me. If I put it upon
the forefinger I can produce whatever I want in a moment:
this palace and all the treasures in it were made in this way.
Finally, if I wear it upon the thumb, of my left hand, that
hand becomes so strong that it can break down rocks and
walls."

"Do let me try," said the Prince, "for I think it must be
your magic that performs all these wonders rather than any
power dwelling in the Ring."

So the Witch Maiden let him wear the ring on the middle
finger of his left hand—and sure enough, no knife would
pierce him whether she stabbed him or he stabbed himself.

"But what did you say would happen if I wore the Ring
on my thumb?" asked the Prince.

"Come down to the courtyard, and I will show you,"
she answered. And when they were there he put the Ring
on his thumb and she bade him strike a great block of stone
with that hand. And immediately he did so, the stone flew
into little pieces.

While they stood laughing at the shattered stone, the
Prince slipped the Ring on to his third finger.

"Now," said the Witch Maiden, "you are invisible until
you take the Ring off." But the Prince had other ideas.
Silently he sped to the furthest end of the courtyard. Then
he took the Ring off his third finger, slipped it on to the
little finger, and soared away into the air like a bird—
leaving the Witch Maiden to lament her folly in ever
trusting the Ring out of her own hands.

Away flew the Prince to the enchanter who had taught him the language of the birds—and the enchanter was able to read the Words of Power engraved on the Ring and instruct the Prince how to wage his war against the Dragon of the North.

The Prince presented himself before the king of the country which the Dragon was at that time laying waste, and said: "Your Majesty, I have come to slay the Dragon and win your daughter as my wife. I can do this, if you will give me all that I need for my task, setting your smiths to work day and night as I may instruct them."

"If you can slay the Dragon," answered the king, "I will give you any powers that you like. Issue what commands you please—and when the Dragon is dead you shall marry the Princess and rule in this land after me."

So the Prince set all the smiths to work. And they made an iron horse with little wheels under each of his feet. And they made a spear six feet long and a foot thick, of solid iron, with a sharp spike at either end. Two chains were fixed to rings in the middle of the spear, and at the other ends of the chains were fastened iron pegs so huge that it took two men to carry them.

When all was ready, the Prince put King Solomon's Ring on his thumb and was able to pick up the spear, chains, pegs and all, with one hand as if it had been a wand of wood.

With the other hand he pushed the iron horse until he came in sight of the Dragon. Then he mounted the horse, and bade the King's soldiers push it. But to his dismay he found that even a hundred of them could not move it, and there seemed nothing to do but push it himself. Moreover when the Dragon saw him and the horse it began to roar so fiercely that the soldiers showed signs of panic.

While he was wondering how he could push the horse and ride on it at the same time, the Prince heard a raven in a tree croaking advice:

"Ride upon the horse, and push the spear against the ground, as if you were pushing off a boat from the land!"

The Prince did so, and found that in this way he could move forward quite easily.

Roaring again, the Dragon gave one of its great hops forward, covering most of the distance which separated him from his victim. The Prince had only a few yards to go before the Dragon could swallow both him and the

horse, and its gigantic jaws, flashing with huge teeth, were already open to receive them.

The Prince trembled with horror and his blood ran cold; but he did not lose his courage, and he knew that if he hesitated for a moment he would himself be lost.

As he reached the Dragon he raised the iron spear upright in his hand and brought it down with all his might straight through the monster's lower jaw. Then, quick as lightning, he sprang from his horse and dodged aside before the Dragon had time to shut his mouth.

Scarcely had he done so when a fearful clap like thunder

told him that the Dragon's jaws had closed upon the spear. Turning, he saw the point sticking out through the Dragon's upper jaw and knew that the other end was fastened firmly to the ground, while the Dragon's teeth were clenched uselessly in the iron horse.

Quickly the Prince drew a great iron mallet from his belt and with it drove the huge pegs at each end of the chain deep into the ground, to make sure that the Dragon could not pull out the spear or move from the spot to which he was pinned.

The Dragon's struggles lasted for three days and three nights, and as he beat his tail on the ground the earth trembled for ten miles in every direction as if there were an earthquake.

As soon as the Dragon could move no more, the Prince picked up a stone which twenty men could not have lifted and struck him so hard upon the head that a moment later he lay lifeless.

Then the Prince married the Princess, and after surviving an attempt made by the Witch Maiden to be revenged on him for the theft of King Solomon's Ring, he became king of the country in which he had killed the Dragon of the North, and lived happily ever after.

The Master Thief and the Dragon

THERE was once a poor peasant in the north of Greece who had two sons. The younger was much the cleverer of the two, and handsomer also, and his brother grew very jealous of him. At last one day when they were alone in the forest the elder brother tied the younger to a tree and left him there to die.

By and by an old hump-backed shepherd passed, driving his flock.

"Whatever are you tied to the tree for?" he asked.

"Because my back was so crooked," answered the young man promptly. "This is the perfect cure. See how straight my back is now! But it all depends on the knots, which few can tie properly!"

"How I wish someone who knew the right knots would tie me to a tree and straighten my back for me!" cried the old shepherd.

"Well, as I'm now cured, I shall be delighted to do the like for you," said the youth. "Just untie me, and I'll have you properly knotted up in two shakes of a lamb's tail."

But as soon as the shepherd was tied to the tree, the youth set off through the forest driving the sheep in front of him. And by the time he reached the other side he had stolen a horse and a herd of oxen, and was soon famous throughout the country as the Master Thief.

In the end, however, he was caught and brought before the King, who said:

"See here, Master Thief, according to the law you should lose your life. But I will spare you if you bring me the Flying Horse which belongs to the Great Dragon."

"That's a mere nothing!" cried the Master Thief, and off he went to the stable where the Horse was tethered. But as soon as he took the Flying Horse by the bridle, it neighed loudly and woke the Dragon who slept in the room just above.

The Thief hid so well, however, that the Dragon could not find him, and went back to bed. As soon as he was asleep, the Thief took the Horse by the bridle once more, and again it neighed so loudly that the Dragon woke: but once more, he could find no sign of any thief.

When the Flying Horse woke him for the third time, and there was no sign of anyone about, the Dragon lost his temper and gave it a good beating. The Flying Horse was so angry at this unfair treatment that when the Master Thief took him by the bridle again, he made no sound and allowed himself to be loosed and led out of the stable.

As soon as they were outside, the Master Thief leapt on the creature's back and flew away, shouting as he went: "Hi, Dragon, hi! If anyone asks where your Flying Horse is, say that the Master Thief has got him!"

The King, however, merely said: "The Flying Horse is all very well, but unless you can bring me the Dragon's bed-spread, I'll have you chopped into a thousand pieces."

"That's easily done!" cried the Master Thief, and off he went to the Dragon's house and climbed on to the roof. When it was dark, he opened the sky-light and let down the chain with the pot-hook on the end of it with which he began to haul up the bed-spread.

But the little bells which were sewn all over it began to ring, and the Dragon woke up, crying: "Wife, you have pulled off all the bed-clothes!" With that he gave such a heave to the bed-spread that the Master Thief fell head first on to the bed, and the Dragon tied him up with the chain and put him in the larder for his Sunday dinner.

Next day the Dragon said to his wife: "I'm just off to see if I can catch anyone coming out of church. But you must stay at home and roast the Master Thief for my dinner!"

But when she untied him, the Master Thief tripped her suddenly so that she fell and broke her neck; and when the Dragon came back from church it was to find his wife roasting in her own oven, and no sign of either the Master Thief or the bed-spread.

The King, however, merely said: "The Dragon's bed-spread is not enough. And the Dragon will now be dangerous. You must bring me the Dragon himself, or else I'll have you cut into a thousand pieces."

"It shall be done," said the Master Thief; and when he had grown a beard and disguised himself as an old man he went to call on the Dragon.

He found that monster in front of his house very busy making a box.

"Good morning, your worship!" said the Master Thief. "Can you spare a morsel of bread for a poor old man?"

"I'll see about that when I've finished my box," snapped the Dragon. "I'm making it to put the Master Thief in—for he has stolen my Flying Horse and cooked my wife."

"He certainly deserves such a fate," croaked the pretended old man. "But he's much too big to fit in that box! He's grown since you last saw him two years ago! He's a very large man now!"

"Nonsense!" cried the Dragon, "it's big enough to hold even me!"

"Well, the villain is nearly as tall as you," said the old man, "and of course if you can get in, he can also. But you'll find it a very tight fit."

"There's plenty of room," growled the Dragon, and to

prove it he climbed into the box, folded his wings carefully, and curled his tail round behind him.

As soon as he was all inside, the Master Thief clapped down the lid and locked it tight. Then he put it on a cart and took it to the King.

The King, however, merely said: "I don't believe a word of it. There's no Dragon in that box! Open it and show me!"

So the Master Thief opened the box just a little way and the Dragon put out his head and swallowed the King in a trice. Then the Master Thief locked up the box, nailed down the lid, married the Princess, and became King himself.

But nobody knows where he put the box with the Dragon in it.

Stan Bolovan and the Dragon

STAN BOLOVAN and his wife lived in a cottage on the edge of a great forest, far from any other houses. For a long time they had no children, and his wife grew sadder and sadder.

But one day Stan Bolovan met a magician who offered to grant him one wish.

"Then give us children," said Stan. "My wife grows sadder each day that we have none."

"How many children?" asked the magician.

"As many as my wife is wishing we had at this moment!" answered Stan.

"It is done!" declared the Magician a moment later. "Go home to your family!"

So Stan Bolovan hastened away until he came to the cottage by the forest. As he drew near he heard the voices of many children; and when he came to the house out poured his family to meet him until he was so overcome that he sat down with a bump and disappeared from sight under the mass of them.

"Good gracious! How many there are! How many!" he gasped.

"Oh, but not one too many!" laughed his wife, coming out with still more children clinging round her. "I wished we had a hundred children—and a hundred children we have!"

All well and good: but how were so many to be fed? As the year wore on this question needed to be answered more and more urgently; and when there was not a scrap of food left in the house, Stan Bolovan said to his wife:

"There is nothing for it but that I should go out into the wide world to seek a fortune, or perish in the attempt."

Next morning, accordingly, he set off into the forest. And he walked and he walked until he came out beyond it on the other side and very nearly to the end of the world.

There he found an old shepherd with a huge flock of sheep and a great herd of cattle. "Can I earn some of these sheep to take away with me to my starving family?" asked Stan Bolovan.

"Easily," answered the shepherd. "You have but to slay or drive away the Dragon who comes each evening. For he takes a ram, a ewe, a lamb, and three fine cows for his dinner. And besides this the milk of seventy-seven ewes so that the Dragoness his mother may bathe in it each night and never grow any older than she is."

Scarcely had he spoken when the great Dragon came flying over the forest, took his evening ration of sheep, cattle and milk, and departed whence he came.

Stan Bolovan did not like the idea of tackling such a terrible fire-breathing creature. But he could see no other way. So he said:

"What will you give me if I rid you of the Dragon for ever?"

"One of every three rams, one of every three ewes and one of every three lambs," was the answer.

"It is a bargain," said Stan Bolovan. "Now tomorrow, when the Dragon comes, leave me to deal with him and you go and hide somewhere well away from here."

When the time came for the Dragon to collect his

evening rations, Stan Bolovan sat himself down on the edge of the sheep-fold and waited.

Presently there came a rushing sound, and the grass was flattened and the bushes rustled with the wind of the monster's wings as it landed.

"Stop and listen to me!" shouted Stan as soon as the Dragon had folded its great wings and was walking towards him, his tongue already licking his great jaws and curved white teeth at the thought of the fine fat cows and sheep waiting for him.

"Who are you, and what do you want?" roared the Dragon.

"I am Stan Bolovan," was the answer. "You've surely heard of me! I eat rocks all night, and by day I feed on the flowers of the mountain. These sheep and cattle are mine now—and if you meddle with them, I'll carve a cross on your back."

"You will have to fight me first," said the Dragon. But he did not sound as fierce as before.

"I fight you!" cried Stan. "Why, I could slay you with one breath!" Then stooping down he picked up a large cheese which lay at his feet and went on:

"Go and get a stone like this out of the river so that we may lose no time in discovering who is the strongest."

The Dragon did as Stan bade him and brought back a stone out of the brook.

"Now," said Stan. "Can you squeeze your stone so hard that buttermilk runs out of it?"

The Dragon took up his stone in one great claw and squeezed it so hard that the sparks flew in every direction and the stone was crushed into powder. But no buttermilk came out of it.

"I thought you were rather a weakling," said Stan contemptuously. "You just watch me!" So saying, he squeezed the cheese until the buttermilk flowed through his fingers.

Now the Dragon, for all his claws and teeth and fiery breath was really a great coward at heart, and not very bright either. "I'd best be getting home," he said, looking anxiously at the pool of buttermilk.

"Not so fast," said Stan severely, "You have still to settle accounts with me for all the sheep and cattle you've taken out of these flocks and herds."

The Dragon was terrified lest Stan should slay him with one breath and bury him among the flowers of the mountain pastures. So, after moving anxiously from one foot to another he said at last:

"Suppose you come home with me to my cave. My mother would be delighted to welcome such a strong man as you, and if you'll serve her for three days she'll pay you seven sacks of ducats each day."

Twenty-one bags of gold were more than Stan Bolovan could resist. He did not waste words, but nodded to the Dragon, and they started along the road.

It was a long way, but when they came to the end of it they found the Dragon's Mother, who was as old as time itself, sitting in her cave expecting them. Stan saw her eyes shining like lamps in the darkness when he reached the door of the cave, and he paused there while the Dragon went in.

"Why have you brought me nothing to eat and no ewes' milk for my bath?" hissed the Dragon's Mother.

"I've brought a man for you to get rid of for me," said the Dragon in a whisper. "He's a terrific fellow who eats rocks and can squeeze buttermilk out of a stone."

"Just leave him to me," she replied. "Tomorrow we'll soon deal with him."

So next day she set Stan Bolovan his first task. "Prove your strength," she said taking down a huge club bound seven times with iron. "See if you can throw this further than my son can."

The Dragon picked up the club as if it had been a little wooden ball for knocking over ninepins, whirled it round his head, and sent it flying over the trees for a good three miles.

Stan and the Dragon went after it, and when they found it the evening had already fallen and the full moon had risen.

Stan picked up the club, which he could only just lift off the ground, and then put it down again. He looked at the moon under his hand for a few minutes, and then sat down on the ground.

"What are you doing?" asked the Dragon.

"Waiting for the moon to get out of my way," answered Stan.

"What do you mean? I don't understand."

"Don't you see that the moon is right in my way? If I throw your club now it will land on the moon, and you'll never see it again."

When he heard this, the Dragon grew cold to the tip of his tail.

"Look here," he said, "I value that club so much (it belonged to my father) that I don't want to risk losing it. I'll give you seven sacks of golden ducats if you give me back the club at once. . . . We'll find a better test."

So Stan Bolovan handed back the club to the Dragon, straining his back rather badly to do so, and then they set out for the cave.

"We're in great danger," the Dragon confided to his Mother later that night. "I only just stopped this monster from flinging my best club right up on to the moon!"

The Dragon's Mother was scared as well this time. But next day she said:

"Go and fetch water, and see who can bring back most before sunset."

The Dragon picked up twelve buffalo skins and brought them back full of water in under ten minutes. Stan Bolovan could scarcely lift one of the skins even when empty. So he sat down by the stream and began slashing at the bank with his knife.

"What are you doing?" asked the Dragon anxiously. "How are you going to bring the water to the cave?"

"How?" exclaimed Stan Bolovan as if greatly surprised. "Why, I'm going to bring the brook itself right into the cave. It will only take me a couple of hours."

"Don't do that!" gasped the Dragon. But it cost him seven more sacks of ducats to keep the stream in its bed.

On the third day the Dragon's Mother sent Stan Bolovan and the Dragon into the forest to see who could bring in the most wood to make faggots for the winter.

In five minutes the Dragon had pulled up more trees than Stan could have cut down in five years and tied them up in neat bundles.

Then Stan set to work with a long rope. He climbed up the biggest tree he could find, tied it to the top, and then fastened it on to the next tree, and so for the whole row.

"What are you doing?" asked the Dragon, more worried than ever before.

"Just to save time and trouble," answered Stan Bolovan. "When I get to the end of the rope one pull will bring up all the trees together. If the rope's long enough, I shall bring in the whole forest for your winter fuel."

It cost the Dragon another seven sacks of golden ducats

to keep the forest where it was; and that night he went to his Mother and burst into tears.

"Woe is us!" howled the Dragon. "This terrible man will soon make slaves of us both. Let's give him all the money he has earned and send him away quickly."

But the Dragon's Mother, who was fond of her gold, said: "No. All you have to do is to wait until he is asleep and then hit him on the head with your club as hard as you can. It's quite easy."

Stan Bolovan had been able to overhear all this, and as soon as the Dragon and his Mother put out their lights he took the pigs' trough, filled it with earth, and put it in his bed with the clothes carefully arranged over it. Then he hid himself underneath and began to snore loudly.

Very soon the Dragon stole softly up to the bed and landed a tremendous blow with his club on the place where Stan Bolovan's head should have been. Stan groaned loudly and stopped snoring, and the Dragon crept quietly away, chuckling gleefully.

As soon as he was gone, Stan Bolovan put the trough back where he had found it, and returned to bed. But he was careful to keep awake for the rest of the night, just in case he should snore in his sleep.

Next morning he strolled into breakfast while the Dragon and his Mother were sharing a salted ox and remarked:

"It would be a good thing to turn a hurricane into this cave for a few hours, I think there must be fleas in it. One bit me on the forehead last night so hard that I still have a small lump there."

"Do you hear that?" whispered the Dragon to his Mother. "He thinks it was only a flea—and I broke my best club on his head!"

So they made ready to send Stan Bolovan on his way, and heaped up all the sacks of golden ducats that he had won for him to carry away with him.

But Stan, who could not have lifted a single one of the sacks off the ground, showed no signs of going.

"I think I'll stay in your service for the next year or so," he said at last. "I shall be ashamed to bring home so little. I know everyone will laugh at me and say: "Just look at Stan Bolovan! In one year he has grown as weak as a dragon!"

At this both the Dragon and the Dragon's Mother uttered loud shrieks of dismay, and began offering him sack after sack of golden ducats, if only he would go at once.

"I see what it is," said Stan Bolovan at last. "You want to get rid of me. Well, I won't stay where I'm not wanted —but I'll only go on condition that you carry all my sacks of golden ducats home for me so that I won't be put to shame before all my friends."

"Willingly!" cried the Dragon, and took up all the dozens and dozens of sacks of golden ducats that Stan Bolovan had won.

Through the forest they went, and at last Stan breathed a sigh of relief as he heard the voices of his children.

"We're nearly there!" he said. "I've got a hundred children, I hope they won't do you any harm; they're a bit inclined to be rough."

The Dragon stopped in terror, and the children—who had had hardly anything to eat since Stan Bolovan left them, came rushing towards him waving their knives and forks and shouting:

"A dragon! You've brought us a dragon for dinner! Three cheers for roast dragon!"

The Dragon took one look, dropped all the sacks of golden ducats and fled for his life. And neither Stan Bolovan nor his hundred children ever saw him again.

The Prince and the Dragon

THERE was once a king who had three sons, fine young men, so fond of hunting that scarcely a day passed without one of them going out to look for game.

One morning the eldest gave chase to a hare which led him up hill and down dale and through the forest until it sought shelter in an old mill beside the river.

The Prince followed it to the very door—and then turned in terror to fly for his life. For inside the mill stood a huge Dragon, breathing smoke and fire. But the Prince could not escape, for he was not across the bridge that led to the mill door before the Dragon's fiery tongue caught him round the waist, plucked him out of the saddle and drew him into the mill; and he was seen no more.

A week passed; the Prince did not return home, and everyone began to grow uneasy. At last the king's second son set out to look for his brother. He had not gone far, however, before up started the hare and led him up hill and down dale and through the forest until it again disappeared into the old mill.

After it went the second Prince, and out of the door came the Dragon's fiery tongue, coiled round his waist, plucked him from the saddle—and he too was seen no more.

Days went by, and the king waited and waited for his

sons to return, but all in vain. His youngest son wished to go in search of them, but for a long time the king would not allow him to go lest he should lose him also. But the young Prince begged so hard and promised to be so careful, that at last the King gave his permission, and ordered the best horse in the royal stables to be saddled for him.

Full of hope, the Prince started on his quest. But no sooner was he outside the city walls than up started the hare and away they went up hill and down dale and through the forest until they came to the old mill.

As before the hare dashed in through the open door: but this Prince did not follow him. Wiser than his brothers, the young man turned back well before he reached the bridge over the river, saying: "There are as good hares in the forest as any that came out of it, and when I have caught them I can come back and look for you."

But he rode about in the edge of the forest, out of sight of anyone in the mill but where he could keep a good eye on it. At last he saw an old woman come slowly out, cross over the bridge and sit down on a fallen tree not far from it.

The Prince then rode cautiously out of the forest and up to where she sat.

"Good day to you, little mother," he said, taking off his hat to her politely. "Can you tell me where I shall find my hare?"

"Good morning, my son," said the old woman. "That was no hare which you followed, but a dragon who has the power of changing his shape, and who has led many men here and then devoured them."

"Alas, then, my brothers have been eaten by the Dragon," cried the Prince.

"They have either been eaten, or put away to be eaten, where you can never find them," answered the old woman. "And my advice to you is to go home at once before the same fate befalls you too."

"Will you not come away with me out of this dreadful place?" asked the Prince. "I can promise you a kind welcome and a comfortable home for the rest of your life."

"I am the Dragon's prisoner," she replied sadly, "and I cannot escape from his spells. But I would help you in any way I can, if only I knew how."

"Then listen to me," said the Prince earnestly. "When the Dragon comes home, ask him where he always goes when he leaves here, and what makes him so strong. Coax the secret from him carefully, and tell me next time I come."

So the Prince went home, and the old woman remained at the mill to coax the Dragon's secret out of him. And she succeeded so well that, after two false answers he gave her the true one:

"My strength lies far away, so far that you could never reach it. Far, far from here is a kingdom, and by its capital city is a lake, and in the lake is a dragon, and inside the dragon is a wild boar, and inside the wild boar is a pigeon, and inside the pigeon a sparrow, and inside the sparrow is my strength."

This sounded as if it must be true, and the old woman sadly gave up coaxing the Dragon, feeling that never, never could anyone take his strength from him.

When she told the Prince, however, he at once set out dressed as a shepherd to look for the far away country where the Dragon's strength lay. He sought in vain until the months of his quest were growing into years; and then at last he came to a large city in a distant kingdom surrounded on three sides by a great lake.

This seemed a likely place, and so he went to the

Emperor who lived there and offered his services as a shepherd.

The Emperor engaged him on the spot, saying: "You may succeed where others have failed. Graze my sheep beyond the lake, but be careful they do not go near the meadows which lie on the edge of the lake itself on this side. They will try to go straight to those meadows, but do not let them—for no sheep which have grazed there have ever come back."

The Prince's heart was filled with hope when he heard this. But he bowed low, promising to guard the sheep as best he could, and set out from the palace to take up his charge.

First of all, however, he went to the market place and bought two greyhounds, a falcon, and a set of pipes. And only then did he drive out the sheep to pasture.

As soon as the sheep saw the lake, they dashed off as fast as their legs would carry them to the green meadows right in front of it. The Prince did not try to stop them: he simply perched his falcon on the branch of a tree, laid his pipes on the grass, and bade the greyhounds sit still. Then rolling up his sleeves and trousers, he waded into the water, crying as he did so:

"Dragon! Dragon! If you are not a coward, come out and fight with me!"

"I am waiting for you, Prince!" came a deep voice from the lake, and a moment later out of the water came the very Dragon of the mill, huge and horrible to see. The Prince sprang upon him and they grappled with each other and fought and wrestled until the sun was high, and it was noonday. Then the Dragon gasped:

"Prince, let me dip my burning head once into the lake, and I will hurl you to the top of the sky."

But the Prince answered: "Ah, ha, my dear Dragon, do not boast too soon! If the Emperor's daughter were only here, and would kiss me on the forehead, I would throw you up higher still!"

At once the Dragon's hold loosened and he sank back into the lake and disappeared under the water.

As soon as it was evening, the Prince washed away all signs of the fight, took his falcon upon his shoulder, his pipes under his arm, and with his greyhounds in front and his flock following after him he set out for the city. As they passed through the streets the people stared in wonder, for never before had any flock returned from the meadow by the lake.

Next morning the Prince set out as before, and all things happened as on the previous day. But the Emperor had commanded two men to follow the Prince unseen, and report on all that he did and all that happened.

They were able to hide quite near the lake, and heard all that the Prince and the Dragon said before the Dragon sunk once more under the water, and the Prince drove his flock safely home from the meadows whence no flock had ever before returned.

Later that night the two men reported all they had seen and heard to the Emperor, and after he had heard it all, he repeated every word to his daughter.

"Tomorrow," he said when he had finished, "you must go with the shepherd to the lake and kiss him on the forehead when he asks for it."

When the Princess heard these words she burst into tears and sobbed: "Will you indeed send me, your only child, to that dreadful lake from which I am quite certain never to return alive?"

"Fear nothing, beloved daughter," said the Emperor,

"all will be well. Many shepherds have gone to the lake, but none of them or their sheep have ever returned. But this one in these two days has fought twice with the Dragon and has escaped without a wound, bringing back with him his flock completely unharmed. So I hope that, with your help, he will kill the Dragon tomorrow and free this land from the monster who has slain so many of our bravest men."

As soon as day dawned the Princess went to the shepherd who laughed with delight when he saw her. But she only wept the more bitterly.

"Do not weep, Heart of Gold," he begged her. "Trust me and fear nothing. Only kiss me on the forehead the moment I ask for it, and all will be well."

So they set out, with the shepherd-prince playing merrily on his pipes until they reached the lake. In an instant the sheep were scattered all over the lush meadows by the waterside. The Prince paid no attention, but placed his falcon on the tree and his pipes on the grass, while he bade his greyhounds lie beside them. Then he rolled up his trousers and his sleeves and waded into the water, saying:

"Dragon! Dragon! If you are not a coward, come out and fight with me again!"

"I am waiting for you, Prince," came the deep voice out of the lake, and a moment later out of the water came the Dragon, huge and horrible to see.

Swiftly he drew near to the bank, and the Prince sprang upon him and they grappled with each other and fought and wrestled until the sun was high and it was noon day.

Then the Dragon gasped: "Prince, let me dip my burning head once into the lake, and I will hurl you to the top of the sky."

But the Prince answered: "Ah-ha, my dear Dragon, do

not boast too soon! If the Emperor's daughter were only here, and would kiss me on the forehead, I would throw you up higher still!"

Hardly had he spoken when the Princess, who had been listening carefully, ran up and kissed him on the forehead. Then the Prince swung the Dragon straight up over the clouds, and when he reached the earth again he broke into a thousand pieces. Out of the pieces there sprang a wild boar, which galloped away. But the Prince called his greyhounds to give chase, and they caught the boar and tore him to pieces. Out of the pieces there sprang a hare, and in a moment the greyhounds were after it and they caught it and killed it and tore it to bits. Out of these bits there came a pigeon which flew swiftly away. But the Prince slipped his falcon which towered straight into the air, swooped upon the bird and brought it to his master. The Prince cut open the dead pigeon and found the sparrow inside, just as the old woman had said he would.

"Now!" cried the Prince, holding the sparrow firmly in his hand, "now you shall tell me where I can find my brothers!"

"Do not hurt me," said the sparrow, "and I will tell you willingly. In the mill where the Dragon used to lurk there are three slender twigs. Cut off these twigs and strike the ground with them, and the iron door of a cellar will open. In the cellar you will find all those whom the Dragon was keeping in ice until he wanted them for his dinner. Breathe three times on each of them, and they will wake as if from sleep—and among them you will find your brothers."

Then the Prince thanked the sparrow and let it fly safely away. He washed himself in the lake, set the falcon on his wrist, the pipes under his arm and with the greyhounds gambolling before and the sheep following after, he took the Princess by the hand and set out for the city.

By the time they reached the palace they were followed by a vast cheering crowd. And when they arrived the Emperor, who had followed unobserved and seen all that had happened, was waiting there to greet them and lead them straight to the chapel royal to be married.

When the wedding and the feast was over, the Prince told them that he was not the poor shepherd he had pretended to be, but a very King's son—and the Emperor rejoiced more than ever. But the Princess felt that she could not have loved him more had he turned out to be Lord of all the Earth.

And when they had freed the two brothers and the other captives from the Dragon's larder, the Prince and Princess settled down to live happily ever after, and in course of time became the best-loved Emperor and Empress that the land had ever known:

The Cock and the Dragon

IN ancient China in the earliest of all days, the Cock had horns on his head. He was a fine bird, beautiful to look upon with his blue-black sickle feathers, his bright red comb and his proud horns.

One day the Dragon came to see him, flying across the sky with his head in one cloud and his tail in another. He was of a green colour, but the edges of his scales glowed red.

Down to earth he flew, settled in the dust near the Cock, and breathed very gently so that no fire should come from his nostrils.

"Honourable Cock," said the Dragon politely in his slow rumbling voice, "I trust that all is well with you?"

"All is very well, noble Dragon," answered the Cock, trying not to look proud that a dragon had come to visit him.

"That is good, honourable Cock," sighed the Dragon, a wisp of smoke curling up from his nostrils.

"May I enquire, noble Dragon, as to the state of your health," said the Cock, not wishing to seem less formal and polite.

"Good, pretty good," replied the Dragon.

"And your fortune, noble Dragon," said the Cock.

"Good," said the Dragon, but he sighed more deeply than ever.

"Can so humble an individual as I do anything to bring
pleasure to so exalted and honourable a personage as yourself, noble Dragon?" asked the Cock, a little anxiously.

"Honourable Cock, you can indeed," said the Dragon.
"I have a great wish to visit the Heavenly Regions and pay
my respects to the Great Heavenly Ones."

"That is a good thought, noble Dragon," said the Cock.

"My great wings will carry me into the Heavenly
Regions," said the Dragon. "But alas, I have no horns."

The Cock looked carefully at the Dragon. "Indeed you
have no horns," he said at last. "But what has this to do

with your visit to the Great Heavenly Ones, noble Dragon?"

"They would mock me and laugh at me," sighed the Dragon. "Without horns I cannot visit the Heavenly Regions. But if you would lend me your horns, Honourable Cock. . . ."

The Dragon paused, and the Cock pecked at the ground uncomfortably.

"If I lent you my horns, noble Dragon, how would I be sure that I would get them back again?" he said at last.

"I have thought of that, honourable Cock," answered the Dragon eagerly. "The Worm is a friend of yours, and a friend of mine. He will tell you how honest I am and that I never break my word. Let us ask him to be my guarantee."

So they both tapped on the ground, and the Worm heard them and came out to see what they wanted.

"Honourable Cock," he said as soon as he heard the story, "the Dragon is sure to bring you back your horns. I will stake my life on it."

This seemed safe enough, and the Cock was rather pleased at the idea of his horns going on a visit to the Heavenly Regions, and at the chance of hearing all about the etiquette of a visit to the Great Heavenly Ones, in case he himself should decide to visit them one day.

So the Cock lent his horns to the Dragon, who looked very fine and imposing with them on his head. Then the Dragon spread his wings and sailed away up into the sky until the Cock and the Worm could see him no longer.

Next morning, almost before it was light, the Cock got up on the farmyard wall, flapped his wings, threw back his head and called loudly: "Give me back my horns! Give me back my horns!" But there was no answer.

That evening he went to consult the Worm, who said: "Honourable Cock, do not worry. If the noble Dragon does not bring back your horns today, he will bring them back tomorrow. He is certainly a creature of honour."

But although every morning the Cock looked up to the sky and crowed loudly: "Give me back my horns!" that "tomorrow" never came.

At last he lost patience, sought out the Worm and gobbled him up. And he gave orders that all proper Cocks after him should eat every worm they could find. It was right, the Cock declared, that worms should suffer for having deceived him—and anyhow they were very good to eat.

Nevertheless, the first thing a cock does every morning, even to this day, is to flap his wings, look up towards the Heavenly Regions to see if the Dragon is coming, and cry: "Give me back my horns! Give me back my horns!"

The Chinese Dragons

ALTHOUGH Dragons played a part in their folk-lore and superstitions for thousands of years, the Chinese seem to have had very few stories about them. Dragons appear usually to have been great but kindly beings, closely connected with the sky, with clouds and storms and the greater wonders of nature.

"Clouds owe their divine character to dragons," wrote Han Yu, who lived about eleven hundred years ago, "dragons do not owe their divinity to clouds. Yet the dragon apart from the clouds would have no means of giving form to his divinity ... Clouds emanate from dragons."

"The chief dragon has his abode in the sky, and all clouds and vapours, winds and rains are under his control," said an even earlier author in a work called the *Yih King*, "He can send rain or withhold it at pleasure, and so all vegetable life depends on him. In the same way the Emperor from his throne watches over the interests of his people and gives to them all those temporal and spiritual blessings without which they would all perish." This is why the Emperors of China sat on a dragon-throne, and they only were allowed to have five-clawed dragons embroidered on their robes.

The great Chinese dictionary *Pan Tsao Kang Mu,* compiled about 1600 A.D., has a long article on Dragons. "The dragon," it tells us from much older sources, "is described as the largest of scaled creatures. Its head is like a camel's, its horns like a deer's, its eyes like a hare's, its ears like a bull's, its neck like a snake's, its belly like a frog's, its scales like a carp's, its claws like an eagle's, and its paws like a tiger's. Its scales number eighty-one, being nine by nine, the extreme odd and lucky number. Its voice is like the beating of a gong. On each side of its mouth are whiskers, under its chin is a bright pearl, under its throat the scales are reversed, on top of its head is the *poh shan* which looks like a wooden foot-rule: without it a dragon cannot go up into the skies. When it breathes the breath forms clouds, sometimes changing into rain, at other times into fire. . . . The dragon comes from an egg. . . .

"It is said that the disposition of the dragon is very fierce, and it is fond of beautiful gems and jade. It is extremely fond of swallow's flesh; it dreads iron, the *mong* plant, the centipede, the leaves of the Pride of India (the azedarac tree) and silk dyed in five different colours. A man therefore who eats swallow's flesh should fear to cross the water. When rain is wanted a swallow should be offered; when floods are to be restrained, then iron; to stir up the dragon the *mong* plant should be employed."

Dragons were not always taken so seriously, however. Their bones were used for many medical purposes: apparently the fossilized bones of prehistoric monsters were dug up in dried river beds, and sometimes skeletons were found in caves.

There was some doubt, however, as to whether dragons could actually die, or not: "All dragons cast off their bodies without actually dying," says one authority. "When a mountain cavern has exposed to view a skeleton head, horns and all, who is to know whether it is a cast off head or whether the dragon has really been killed?" asked Tsung Shih.

But a work called the *I-ki* seems to put the matter of whether or not dragons die beyond a doubt: "In the time of the Emperor Hwo of the Han Dynasty (about B.C. 100) during a heavy shower a dragon fell in the palace grounds, which the Emperor ordered to be made into soup and given to his Ministers."

And, as if to clinch the matter, Lu Kuei-meng, a hermit living in the ninth century A.D. told the following story:

"The name of Dragon-Keeper was once given to a man who was greatly interested in dragons, knew their tastes and habits, and actually kept a pair in captivity.

"Thinking he was allowing them to follow their natural instincts, Mr. Dragon-Keeper gave his pets a pond in the palace garden to live in—though a hundred rivers and the four oceans are not enough for dragons to sport in. And he fed them with choice meat and titbits—though the great whales in all the seas are not enough to satisfy the appetites of the dragon-kind. Nevertheless, these two dragons grew tame and lazy, and were quite content to remain where they were.

"One morning a wild dragon flew by, and they called to him in amazement, saying: "Whatever are you doing up there? It must be a dreadful existence, flying about all the time looking for food: come and live comfortably down here with us."

"The wild dragon tossed his head proudly and laughed, crying: 'What, live all cramped up in a wretched little pool like you? I am a dragon, with crest and horns and shining scales! I have the power of lying hidden in the waters or of flying through the sky; mine is the spirit which blows the clouds along and rides upon the wind; it is my business to parch the proud and give drink to the thirsty. I rest in the regions outside the bounds of space, I go wherever I like, in whatever form I please. Is not this true happiness? As for you, if you are satisfied to live in a puddle, no better than earthworms, interested only in getting plenty to eat and drink without any efforts of your own—well, though you look like dragons, I say you are none. He who fawns upon mankind, hoping to profit thereby, deludes himself: sooner or later you will be killed and skinned and made into mincemeat. I pity you and would help you to escape—and instead of taking advantage of your last chance, you ask me to come and share your fate! No indeed, you cannot now escape!'

"So saying the wild dragon spread his wings and flew away. But what he said was true, for very soon the two dragons found themselves made into mincemeat and served up on the Emperor's table."

PART FOUR

Dragons of Later Days

The Red Cross Knight and the Dragon

Edmund Spenser in "The Faerie Queene" (1590) used the legend of St. George, Sabra and the Dragon in his Book One as the basis for the allegorical story of how the Red Cross Knight saved Una from the Dragon of Sin. Spenser's superb romantic epic is much too long even for a single Canto to be included here: but he could not be left out altogether, and a few stanzas have been inserted into Mary MacLeod's retelling of that last fight.

AT last Una and the Knight came to Una's kingdom, where her parents were held captive, and all the land lay wasted by the terrible Dragon. As they drew near their journey's end, Una began to cheer her companion with brave words.

"Dear Knight," she said, "who for my sake have suffered all these sorrows, may Heaven reward you for your weary toil! Now we have come to my own country, and the place where all our perils dwell. This is the haunt of the horrible monster, therefore be well on your guard and ready for the foe. Call up all your courage, and do better than you have ever done before, so that hereafter you shall be renowned above all knights on earth."

At this moment they heard a hideous roaring sound, which filled the air and almost shook the solid earth. Soon they saw the dreadful Dragon where he lay stretched on the sunny side of a great hill. Directly he caught sight of the glittering armour of the Knight, he quickly roused himself, and hastened towards them.

The Red Cross Knight bade Una go to a hill at some distance, from where she might behold the battle and be safe from danger.

By this, the dreadful Beast drew nigh to hand,
Halfe flying and halfe footing in his haste,
That with his largenesse measured much land,
And made wide shadow under his huge waste,
As mountaine doth the valley overcaste.
Approaching nigh, he reared high afore
His body monstrous, horrible, and vaste;
Which, to increase his wondrous greatnes more,
Was swoln with wrath and poyson, and with bloody
   gore;

And over all with brasen scales was armd,
Like plated cote of steele, so couched neare
That nought mote perce; ne might his corse bee harmd
With dint of swerd, nor push of pointed speare:
Which as an Eagle, seeing pray appeare,
His aery plumes doth rouze, full rudely dight;
So shaked he, that horror was to heare;
For as the clashing of an Armor bright,
Such noyse his rouzed scales did send unto the Knight.

His flaggy winges, when forth he did display,
Were like two sayles, in which the hollow wynd
Is gathered full, and worketh speedy way:
And eke the pennes, that did his pineons bynd,
Were like mayne-yardes with flying canvas lynd;
With which whenas him list the ayre to beat,

And there by force unwonted passage fynd,
The cloudes before him fledd for terror great,
And all the hevens stood still amazed with his threat.

His huge long tayle, wownd up in hundred foldes,
Does overspred his long bras-scaly back,
Whose wreathed boughtes when ever he unfoldes,
And thick entangled knots adown does slack,
Bespotted as with shieldes of red and blacke,
It sweepeth all the land behind him farre,
And of three furlongs does but little lacke;
And at the point two stinges in fixed arre,
Both deadly sharp, that sharpest steele exceeden farre.

But stinges and sharpest steele did far exceed
The sharpnesse of his cruel rending clawes:
Dead was it sure, as sure as death in deed,
Whatever thing doth touch his ravenous pawes,
Or what within his reach he ever drawes.
But his most hideous head my tongue to tell
Does tremble; for his deepe devouring jawes
Wyde gaped, like the griesly mouth of hell,
Through which into his darke abysse all ravin fell.

And, that more wondrous was, in either jaw
Three ranckes of yron teeth enraunged were,
In which yett trickling blood and gobbets raw,
Of late devoured bodies did appeare,
The sight thereof bredd cold congealed feare;
Which to increase, and all at once to kill,
A cloud of smothering smoke, and sulphure seare,
Out of his stinking gorge forth steemed still,
That all the ayre about with smoke and stench did fill.

His blazing eyes, like two bright shining shieldes,
Did burne with wrath, and sparkled living fyre:
As two broad Beacons, set in open fieldes,
Send forth their flames far off to every shyre,
And warning give that enimies conspyre
With fire and sword the region to invade:
So flam'd his eyne with rage and rancorous yre;
But far within, as in a hollow glade,
Those glaring lampes were sett that made a dreadfull
    shade.

Such was the terrible monster with whom the Red Cross
Knight had now to do battle.

All day they fought; and when evening came, the
Knight was quite worn out and almost defeated. As it
chanced, however, close by was a spring, the waters of
which possessed a wonderful gift of healing. The Knight
was driven backwards and fell into this well. The Dragon
clapped his wings in triumph, for he thought he had gained
the victory. But so great was the power of the water in
this well that although the Knight's own strength was
utterly exhausted, yet he rose out of it refreshed and
vigorous. The dawn of the next day found him stronger
than ever, and ready for battle.

The name of the spring was called the Well of Life.

All through the second day the battle lasted, and again,
when evening came, the Knight was almost defeated. But
this night he rested under a beautiful tree laden with goodly
fruit; the name of the tree was the Tree of Life. From it
flowed, as from a well, a trickling stream of balm, a perfect cure for all ills, and whoever ate of its fruit attained to
everlasting life.

The strength of the Red Cross Knight alone would never have been sufficient to overcome the terrible Dragon of Sin, but the water of the Well of Life, and balm from the Tree of Life, gave him a power that nothing could resist.

Then freshly up arose the doughty Knight,
All healed of his hurts and woundes wide,
And did himselfe to battaile ready dight;
Whose early foe awaiting him beside
To have devoured, so soone as day he spyde,
When now he saw himself so freshly reare,
As if late fight had nought him damnifyde,
He woxe dismaid, and gan his fate to feare:
Nathlesse with wonted rage he him advaunced neare.

And in his first encounter, gaping wyde,
He thought attonce him to have swallowd quight,
And rusht upon him with outragious pryde;
Who him rencountring fierce, as hauke in flight,
Perforce rebutted backe. The weapon bright,
Taking advantage of his open jaw,
Ran through his mouth with so importune might,
That deepe emperst his darksom hollow maw,
And, back retyrd, his life blood forth with all did draw.

So downe he fell, and forth his life did breath,
That vanisht into smoke and cloudes swift;
So downe he fell, that th' earth him underneath
Did grone, as feeble so great load to lift;
So downe he fell, as an huge rocky clift,
Whose false foundacion waves have washt away,

With dreadful poyse is from the mayneland rift,
And rolling downe great Neptune doth dismay:
So downe he fell, and like an heaped mountaine lay.

The Knight himselfe even trembled at his fall,
So huge and horrible a masse it seemd;
And his deare Lady, that beheld it all,
Durst not approch for dread which she misdeemd;
But yet at last, whenas the direfull feend
She saw not stirre, off-shaking vaine affright
She nigher drew, and saw that joyous end:
Then God she praysd, and thankt her faithfull Knight,
That had atchievde so great a conquest by his might.

The sun had scarcely risen on the third day, when the
watchman on the walls of the brazen tower saw the death
of the Dragon. He hastily called to the captive King and
Queen who, coming forth, ordered the tidings of peace
and joy to be proclaimed through the whole land.

Then all the trumpets sounded for victory, and the
people came flocking as to a great feast, rejoicing at the fall
of the cruel enemy, from whose bondage they were now
free. . . .

The King gave goodly gifts of gold and ivory to his
brave champion the Red Cross Knight, and thanked him a
thousand times for all that he had done.

And to the Knight his daughter deare he tyde
With sacred rites and vowes for ever to abyde.

The Shepherd of the Giant Mountains

This is a long narrative poem, first published in 1846, by the minor poetess Menella Bute Smedley, based on a story by the German romance and fairy tale writer Fouqué, best known for his "Undine". Miss Smedley was a cousin and friend of Lewis Carroll, and this poem may have given him the idea for "Jabberwocky" the first version of which was written after a New Year Party at which she was present. The monster is here called a Griffin, but the picture (which fascinated Rudyard Kipling as a small boy) shows an indubitable Dragon. The poem is too long and rambling to include complete, so I have quoted the best bits from it and linked them with a short prose narrative.

Love ye to listen to a goodly tale,
Full of simplicity, yet full of marvel,
Brightness, and beauty, like the days of old?
Then follow me
Back through full many a hoary century!
Come to the Giant Mountains,
Which separate Silesia from Bohemia—
Deep in the deepest of their shadowy glens,
Just at the hour when eve her dewy mantle,
Streaked with a few faint lines of sunny gold,
Spreads forth, admonishing to sweet repose!
But in the mountain-woods
The shepherds roam in terror to and fro,
Gaze upward fearfully, and, if a sound
Cleave the grey clouds above like rushing wings,
Dive under bush and reed, and murmur hoarsely,
"The Griffin! ah the Griffin! God defend us!"

Only one of the shepherds seemed uninterested in the
Griffin, and this was young Gottschalk, who calmly went
on playing his pipe as if no winged monster had flown by.
The other shepherds were annoyed with him for his
seeming indifference, but one old man said at length:

"Well, well, the peril's over for today;
The Griffin's in her nest, an there she feeds
A brood of growing griffins like herself,
Who shall, in days to come, be our destruction."
Herewith the garrulous old man began
A piteous tale of plunder and distress,
Reckoning the numbers of the monster's prey
"I too," young Gottschalk, with a nod, replied—
"I too, have lost the fairest of my flock;
Six of my lambs the ravening beast hath seized."

The Griffin being safely in her nest, the rest of the evening
was spent by the shepherds in song and dance.
    But not many days later there came a herald with a
proclamation:

"Greetings and favour from our Lord the Duke
To every Christian dweller in the land!
Whereas 'tis known to many, that for long
A monstrous Griffin hath devoured the flocks
And scared the trembling shepherds, unopposed
Spreading its devastation o'er the plains;
Our gracious master, to the valiant man
Who shall subdue and slay this hideous monster,
Offers, as prize and pledge of victory,
The hand of Adiltrude, his only daughter,
So peerless in her beauty and her grace.
Up, warriors, to the fight! Arm, heroes, arm!"

Naturally this challenge inspired Gottschalk to try his fortune against the Griffin, and presently he set forth to find its home and decide on a plan of campaign.

He discovered that the Griffin had its nest on the top of a gigantic oak tree, and by climbing a cliff nearby was able to look down on to it.

The Griffin stoops—doubtless her nest is here,
In the tall branches of yon monstrous oak.
Ha! hark how suddenly the ancient branches
Do stir and rustle!
Hark to that shrill and hissing sound, and see
How from the leaves a group of scaly throats,
With various hues all hideous in their brightness,
Stretch forth to meet their booty-laden mother,
Who hisses her shrill answer of grim joy.
And now begins the banquet (close at hand
The shepherd, peering from his giddy height,
Looks sheer upon the horrors of the nest);
Now do the bones of strangled oxen crack
Like dry boughs smitten with the axe, and now
The greedy griffin-brood break off their revel
To quarrel for the dainties; curl and twist
Their ghastly necks in many a filthy knot,
Biting each other, and with barbed claws
Clutching and griping at each other's throats,
The aged Griffin, barbarous peace-maker,
Lashes her angry children with her wings;
Wild howl the savage brood, and then again
Renew their feasting, fight, and howl again,
While, from the oak's tall stem,
Gushes a hideous stream of mingled blood
From strife and banquet poured—from slain and slayer.

Reeling with horror, Gottschalk well nigh sank
From his tall crag, but manned himself, and grasped
The side, and firmly stood; and having seen
All that he sought, with slow and cautious steps
Clombe downwards unperceived, and paused once more,
Safe for the present, in the peaceful vale.

And the very next day, Gottschalk set forth to do battle
with the Griffin.

Now, with his herdsman's staff, iron-tipped and
    sharpened
Like a good battle-axe, upon his shoulder,
Gottschalk sets forth upon his dreary way,
Beneath the burning noon,
When, as he knows, the monster leaves her nest,
And seeks her prey amid the distant plains.

As he drew near to the terrible tree, Gottschalk was
seized with sudden fear, and paused and stood in thought,
fighting with himself. Then at length he fell upon his
knees and prayed for strength. And presently a great calm
determination to serve his prince and save his friends and
fellow-countrymen seemed to flow over him. He rose
from his knees, looked up at the tree and cried:

"Hideous and spiteful griffin-brood, I see
Your grim looks watching me, I hear your voices
Lift up their shrill and hissing scream, I know ye!
Ye crave my bones to grace your ghastly banquet!
I care not!
I love to see ye look so terrible,
Else might it pain me thus with fire to burn

Your living forms! Now to the work of death!"
  A branch he kindles on a lofty stem,
And lifts it up with toil to touch the nest.
Ha, how the dry bark catches, flames, and flares!
The oak itself, so often steeped in blood,
That its parched leaves no longer greenly flourish,
And its stiff boughs are hollow, dried and dead—
The oak itself is kindled by the fire—
It hisses, it rustles, it cracks,

And through the tumult of the rising flames
Pierce the shrill howlings of the tortured brood.
Far on her bloody way
The mother Griffin heard,
And measuring a league with every stroke
Of her colossal wings, she rushes upward,
Shadowing the mountain with a fearful darkness.
Then Gottschalk thought, "the dream of life is past!"
And gave his soul into the hands of God.
But, heedless of revenge,
The Griffin strikes and strives to quench the flame
With her huge wings; strikes with such eager fury,
That Gottschalk marvelled how so fierce a monster
Should yet preserve her children by the risk
Of her own life. In vain! The grisly brood
Lie scorched and stifled in the pangs of death;
And lo! the flame hath caught the Griffin's wings,
As if in thirst for vengeance!
The reeling monster falls upon the grass,
Now, shepherd, now! Where is thy ready staff?
Now! Lose no moment! For the wrathful beast,
Frantic with rage and pain, hath reared itself
On its broad feet, and stands, half-tottering,
But dreadful still, and eager for the fight:
Then had the hapless youth been crushed to nothing,
But that he lifted up his heart to God,
And that a vision of inspiring beauty
Rose on his soul, and bade him not despair!
Stroke upon stroke he hurls against the foe:
He stabs it in the fiery eye—the beast
Rears in wild rage, then, quick as thought, the staff
Pierces its undefended breast, and sinks,
Sure, deep, and deadly, in the ruthless heart!

It roars as with the congregated voices
Of thousand oxen; reels, and strikes its wings
Once more, with impotent fury, on the earth—
And all is over!
The terror of the land lies stiff in death!

Once the Griffin was dead, Gottschalk had the corpse dragged to the palace and claimed his prize, the hand of the lovely Adiltrude.

Both the Duke and Adiltrude were only too eager to welcome Gottschalk into their family, and the Duke began by presenting him with as much land as he could drive his flock of sheep round in one day.

But Gottschalk would not take his bride until he had gone forth adventuring and been made a knight. And on his return he was forced to fight and defeat the jealous Sir Baldwin who envied him his position as heir to the Duke and had hoped to marry Lady Adiltrude himself.

When the fight was ended, and Gottschalk had proved himself yet again to be worthy both of the order of knighthood and the hand of his lady,

The Duke cried, stooping from his balcony,
In gratulating tones,
"Come to my heart, my true and gallant son!"

Jabberwocky

LEWIS CARROLL

Was the Jabberwock a Dragon? Well, the Snark was a Boojum, you see—so why not? Tenniel's famous picture of "the Jabberwock with eyes of flame" certainly shows a very dragonish creature whiffling through the tulgey woods— and he was at least as much a Dragon as the Griffin in "The Shepherd of the Giant Mountains" who seems to have inspired him.

'Twas brillig, and the slithy toves
   Did gyre and gimble in the wabe;
All mimsy were the borogoves,
   And the mome raths outgrabe.

"Beware the Jabberwock, my son!
   The jaws that bite, the claws that catch!
Beware the Jubjub bird, and shun
   The frumious Bandersnatch!"

He took his vorpal sword in hand:
   Long time the manxome foe he sought—
So rested he by the Tumtum tree,
   And stood awhile in thought.

And, as in uffish thought he stood,
   The Jabberwock, with eyes of flame,
Came whiffling through the tulgey wood,
   And burbled as it came!

One, two! One, two! And through and through
   The vorpal blade went snicker-snack!
He left it dead, and with its head
   He went galumphing back.

"And hast thou slain the Jabberwock?
   Come to my arms, my beamish boy!
O frabjous day! Callooh! Callay!"
   He chortled in his joy.

'Twas brillig, and the slithy toves
   Did gyre and gimble in the wabe:
All mimsy were the borogoves,
   And the mome raths outgrabe.

The Lady Dragonissa

ANDREW LANG

The collector and editor of the twelve coloured Fairy Books that range from Blue to Lilac was also the author of one of the best of all invented fairy stories, "Prince Prigio". This contains a splendid fight between a Fire Dragon and an Ice Dragon—but it would spoil a splendid book to take a bit out of it: you must read "Prince Prigio" as a whole. But Andrew Lang added an incident out of the early history of the Royal Family of Pantouflia when he reprinted the stories of Prince Prigio and of his son Prince Ricardo in one volume—and here it is.

ABOUT the ancient kingdom of Pantouflia very little is known. The natives speak German; but the Royal Family, as usual, was of foreign origin. Just as England had Norman, Scottish, and, at present, a line of German monarchs, so the kings of Pantouflia are descended from an old Greek family, the Hypnotidae, who came to Pantouflia during the Crusades. They wanted, they explained, not to be troubled with the Crusades, which they thought very injudicious and tiresome. The Crest of the regal house is a Dormouse, dormant, proper, on a field vert, and the Motto, when translated out of the original Greek, means, *Anything for a Quiet Life.*

It may surprise the young reader that princes like Prigio and Ricardo, whose feet were ever in the stirrup, and whose lances were always in rest, should have descended from the family of the Hypnotidae, who were remarkedly lazy and peaceful. But these heroes doubtless inherited the spirit of

their great ancestress, whose story is necessary to be known. On leaving his native realm during the Crusades, in search of some secure asylum, the founder of the Pantouflian monarchy landed in the island of Cyprus, where, during the noontide heat, he lay down to sleep in a cave. Now in this cave dwelt a dragon of enormous size and unamiable character. What was the horror of the exiled prince when he was aroused from slumber by the fiery breath of the dragon, and felt its scaly coils about him!

"Oh, hang your practical jokes!" exclaimed the prince, imagining that some of his courtiers were playing a prank on him.

"Do you call *this* a joke?" asked the dragon, twisting its forked tail into a line with his royal highness's eye.

"Do take that thing away," said the prince, "and let a man have his nap peacefully."

"KISS ME!" cried the dragon, which had already devoured many gallant knights for declining to kiss it.

"Give you a kiss," murmured the prince; "Oh, certainly, if that's all! *Anything for a quiet life.*"

So saying, he kissed the dragon, which instantly became a most beautiful princess; for she had lain enchanted as a dragon, by a wicked magician, till somebody should be bold enough to kiss her.

"My love! my hero! my lord! how long I have waited for thee; and now I am eternally thine own!"

So murmured, in the most affectionate accents, the Lady Dragonissa, as she was now called.

Though wedded to a bachelor life, the prince was much too well-bred to make any remonstrance.

The Lady Dragonissa, a female of extraordinary spirit, energy, and ambition, took command of him and his followers, conducted them up the Danube, seized a principality whose lord had gone crusading, set her husband on the throne, and became in course of time the mother of a little prince, who, again, was great, great, great, great grandfather of our Prince Prigio.

From this adventurous Lady Dragonissa, Prince Prigio derived his character for gallantry. But her husband, it was said, was often heard to remark, by a slight change of his family motto:

"*Anything for a Quiet Wife!*"

The Fiery Dragon

E. NESBIT

THE little white Princess always woke in her little white bed when the starlings began to chatter in the pearl-grey morning. As soon as the woods were awake, she used to run up the twisting turret-stairs with her little bare feet, and stand on the top of the tower in her white bed-gown, and kiss her hands to the sun and to the woods and to the sleeping town, and say: "Good morning, pretty world!"

Then she would run down the cold stone steps and dress herself in her short skirt and her cap and apron, and begin the day's work. She swept the rooms and made the breakfast, she washed the dishes and she scoured the pans, and all this she did because she was a real Princess. For of all who should have served her, only one remained faithful—her old nurse, who had lived with her in the tower all the Princess's life. And, now the nurse was old and feeble, the Princess would not let her work any more, but did all the housework herself while nurse sat still and did the sewing, because this was a real Princess with a skin like milk, and hair like flax and a heart like gold.

Her name was Sabrinetta, and her grandmother was Sabra, who married St. George after he had killed the dragon, and by real rights all the country belonged to her: the woods that stretched away to the mountains, and the downs that sloped down to the sea, and the pretty fields of corn and maize and rye, the olive orchards and the vineyards, and the little town itself with its towers and its turrets, its steep roofs and strange windows, that nestled in the hollow between the sea where the whirlpool was and the mountains, white with snow and rosy with sunrise.

But when her father and mother died, leaving her cousin to take care of the kingdom till she grew up, he, being a very evil Prince, had taken everything away from her, and all the people had followed him, and now nothing was left her of all her possessions except the great dragon-proof tower that her grandfather, St. George, had built, and of all who should have been her servants, only the good nurse.

And this was why Sabrinetta was the first person in all the land to get a glimpse of the wonder.

Early, early, early, while all the townspeople were fast asleep, she ran up the turret-steps and looked out over the field, and at the other side of the field there is a green-ferny ditch and a rose-thorny hedge, and then comes the wood. And as Sabrinetta stood on her tower she saw a shaking and a twisting of the rose-thorny hedge, and then something very bright and shining wriggled out through it into the ferny ditch and back again. It only came out for a minute, but she saw it quite plainly, and she said to herself: "Dear me, what a curious, shiny, bright-looking creature! If it were bigger, and if I didn't know that there have been no fabulous monsters for quite a long time now, I should almost think it was a dragon."

The thing, whatever it was, did look rather like a dragon—but then it was too small; and it looked rather like a lizard—only then it was too big. It was about as long as a hearthrug.

"I wish it had not been in such a hurry to get back into the wood," said Sabrinetta. "Of course, it's quite safe for me, in my dragon-proof tower; but if it is a dragon, it's quite big enough to eat people, and today's the first of May, and the children go out to get flowers in the wood."

When Sabrinetta had done the housework (she did not leave so much as a speck of dust anywhere, even in the corneriest corner of the winding stair) she put on her milk-white silky gown with the moon-daisies worked on it, and went up to the top of her tower again.

Across the fields troops of children were going out to gather the may, and the sound of their laughter and singing came up to the top of the tower.

"I do hope it *wasn't* a dragon," said Sabrinetta.

The children went by twos and by threes and by tens and by twenties, and the red and blue and yellow and white of their frocks were scattered on the green of the field.

"It's like a green silk mantle worked with flowers," said the Princess, smiling.

By twos and by threes, by tens and by twenties, the children vanished into the wood, till the mantle of the field was left plain green once more.

"All the embroidery is unpicked," said the Princess, sighing.

The sun shone, and the sky was blue, and the fields were quite green, and all the flowers were very bright indeed, because it was May Day.

Then quite suddenly a cloud passed over the sun, and the silence was broken by shrieks from afar off; and, like a many-coloured torrent, all the children burst from the wood, and rushed, a red and blue and yellow and white wave, across the field, screaming as they ran. Their voices came up to the Princess on her tower, and she heard the words threaded on their screams, like beads on sharp needles:

"The dragon, the dragon, the dragon! Open the gates! The dragon is coming! The fiery dragon!"

And they swept across the field and into the gate of the town, and the Princess heard the gate bang, and the children were out of sight—but on the other side of the field the rosethorns crackled and smashed in the hedge, and something very large and glaring and horrible trampled the ferns in the ditch for one moment before it hid itself again in the covert of the wood.

The Princess went down and told her nurse, and the nurse at once locked the great door of the tower and put the key in her pocket.

"Let them take care of themselves," she said, when the Princess begged to be allowed to go out and help to take care of the children.

"My business is to take care of you, my precious, and I'm going to do it. Old as I am, I can turn a key still."

So Sabrinetta went up again to the top of her tower, and cried whenever she thought of the children and the fiery dragon. For she knew, of course, that the gates of the town were not dragon-proof, and that the dragon could just walk in whenever he liked.

The children ran straight to the palace, where the Prince was cracking his hunting-whip down at the kennels, and told him what had happened.

"Good sport," said the Prince, and he ordered out his pack of hippopotamuses at once. It was his custom to hunt big game with hippopotamuses, and people would not have minded that so much—but he would swagger about in the streets of the town with his pack yelping and

gambolling at his heels, and, when he did that, the green-grocer, who had his stall in the market-place, always regretted it; and the crockery merchant, who spread his wares on the pavement, was ruined for life every time the Prince chose to show off his pack.

The Prince rode out of the town with his hippopotamuses trotting and frisking behind him, and people got inside their houses as quickly as they could when they heard the voices of his pack and the blowing of his horn. The pack squeezed through the town gates and off across country to hunt the dragon. Few of you who have not seen a pack of hippopotamuses in full cry will be able to imagine at all what the hunt was like. To begin with, hippopotamuses do not bay like hounds: they grunt like pigs, and their grunt is very big and fierce. Then, of course, no one expects hippopotamuses to jump. They just crash through the hedges and lumber through the standing corn, doing serious injury to the crops, and annoying the farmers very much. All the hippopotamuses had collars with their name and address on, but when the farmers called at the palace to complain of the injury to their standing crops, the Prince always said it served them right for leaving their crops standing about in people's way, and he never paid anything at all.

So now, when he and his pack went out, several people in the town whispered, "I wish the dragon would eat *him*"—which was very wrong of them, no doubt, but then he was such a very nasty Prince.

They hunted by field, and they hunted by wold; they drew the woods blank, and the scent didn't lie on the down at all. The dragon was shy, and would not show himself.

But just as the Prince was beginning to think there was no dragon at all, but only a cock and bull, his favourite old hippopotamus gave tongue. The Prince blew his horn and shouted: "Tally ho! Hark forward! Tantivy!" and the whole pack charged down-hill towards the hollow by the wood. For there, plain to be seen, was the dragon, as big as a barge, glowing like a furnace, and spitting fire and showing his shining teeth.

"The hunt is up!" cried the Prince. And, indeed, it was. For the dragon—instead of behaving as a quarry should, and running away—ran straight at the pack, and the Prince on his elephant had the mortification of seeing his prize pack swallowed up one by one in the twinkling of an eye, by the dragon they had come out to hunt. The dragon swallowed all the hippopotamuses just as a dog swallows bits of meat. It was a shocking sight. Of the whole of the pack that had come out sporting so merrily to the music of the horn, now not even a puppy-hippopotamus was left, and the dragon was looking anxiously round to see if he had forgotten anything.

The Prince slipped off his elephant on the other side, and ran into the thickest part of the wood. He hoped the dragon could not break through the bushes there, since they were very strong and close. He went crawling on hands and knees in a most un-Prince-like way, and at last, finding a hollow tree, he crept into it. The wood was very still—no crashing of branches and no smell of burning came to alarm the Prince. He drained the silver hunting-bottle slung from his shoulder, and stretched his legs in the hollow tree. He never shed a single tear for his poor tame hippopotamuses who had eaten from his hand, and followed him faithfully in all the pleasures of the chase for so many years. For he was a false Prince, with a skin like leather and hair like hearth-brushes, and a heart like a stone. He never shed a tear, but he just went to sleep. When he awoke it was dark. He crept out of the tree and rubbed his eyes. The wood was black about him, but there was a red glow in a dell close by, and it was a fire of sticks, and beside it sat a ragged youth with long, yellow hair; all round lay sleeping forms which breathed heavily.

"Who are you?" said the Prince.

"I'm Elfinn, the pig-keeper," said the ragged youth. "And who are you?"

"I'm Tiresome, the Prince," said the other.

"And what are you doing out of your palace at this time of night? "asked the pig-keeper, severely.

"I've been hunting," said the Prince.

The pig-keeper laughed. "Oh, it was you I saw, then? A good hunt, wasn't it? My pigs and I were looking on."

All the sleeping forms grunted and snored, and the

Prince saw that they were pigs: he knew it by their manners.

"If you had known as much as I do," Elfinn went on, "you might have saved your pack."

"What do you mean?" said Tiresome.

"Why, the dragon," said Elfinn. "You went out at the wrong time of day. The dragon should be hunted at *night*."

"No, thank you," said the Prince, with a shudder. "A daylight hunt is quite good enough for me, you silly pig-keeper."

"Oh, well," said Elfinn, "do as you like about it—the dragon will come and hunt *you* tomorrow, as likely as not. I don't care if he does, you silly Prince."

"You're very rude," said Tiresome.

"Oh, no, only truthful," said Elfinn.

"Well, tell me the truth, then. What is it that if I had known as much as you do about I shouldn't have lost my hippopotamuses?"

"You don't speak very good English," said Elfinn; "but, come, what will you give me if I tell you?"

"If you tell me what?" said the tiresome Prince.

"What you want to know."

"I don't want to know anything," said Prince Tiresome.

"Then you're more of a silly even than I thought," said Elfinn. "Don't you want to know how to settle the dragon before he settles you?"

"It might be as well," the Prince admitted.

"Well, I haven't much patience at any time," said Elfinn, "and now I can assure you that there's very little left. What will you give me if I tell you?"

"Half my kingdom," said the Prince, "and my cousin's hand in marriage."

"Done," said the pig-keeper; "here goes! *The dragon grows small at nights!* He sleeps under the root of this tree. I use him to light my fire with."

And, sure enough, there under the trees was the dragon on a nest of scorched moss, and he was about as long as your finger.

"How can I kill him?" asked the Prince.

"I don't know that you *can* kill him," said Elfinn; "but you can take him away if you've brought anything to put him in. That bottle of yours would do."

So between them they managed, with bits of stick and by singeing their fingers a little, to poke and shove the dragon till they made it creep into the silver hunting-bottle and then the Prince screwed on the top tight.

"Now we've got him," said Elfinn, "let's take him home and put Solomon's seal on the mouth of the bottle, and then he'll be safe enough. Come along—we'll divide up the kingdom tomorrow, and then I shall have some money to buy fine clothes to go courting in."

But when the wicked Prince made promises he did not make them to keep.

"Go on with you! What do you mean?" he said. "*I* found the dragon and I've imprisoned him. I never said a word about courtings or kingdoms. If you say I did, I shall cut your head off at once." And he drew his sword.

"All right," said Elfinn, shrugging his shoulders. "I'm better off than you are, anyhow."

"What do you mean?" spluttered the Prince.

"Why, you've only got a kingdom (and a dragon), but I've got clean hands (and five-and-seventy fine black pigs)."

So Elfinn sat down again by his fire, and the Prince went home and told his Parliament how clever and brave he had been, and though he woke them up on purpose to tell them, they were not angry, but said:

"You are indeed brave and clever." For they knew what happened to people with whom the Prince was not pleased.

Then the Prime Minister solemnly put Solomon's seal on the mouth of the bottle, and the bottle was put in the treasury, which was made of solid copper, with walls as thick as Waterloo Bridge.

The bottle was set down among the sacks of gold, and the junior secretary to the junior clerk of the last Lord of the Treasury was appointed to sit up all night with it, and see if anything happened. The junior secretary had never seen a dragon, and what was more, he did not believe the Prince had ever seen a dragon either. The Prince had never been a really truthful boy, and it would have been just like him to bring home a bottle with nothing in it, and then to pretend that there was a dragon inside. So the junior secretary did not at all mind being left. They gave him the key, and when everyone in the town had gone back to bed he let in some of the junior secretaries from other Government departments, and they had a jolly game of hide-and-seek among the sacks of gold, and played marbles with the diamonds and rubies and pearls in the big ivory chests.

They enjoyed themselves very much, but by-and-by the copper treasury began to get warmer and warmer, and suddenly the junior secretary cried out, "Look at the bottle!"

The bottle sealed with Solomon's seal had swollen to three times its proper size, and seemed to be nearly red hot, and the air got warmer and warmer and the bottle bigger and bigger, till all the junior secretaries agreed that the place was too hot to hold them, and out they went, tumbling

over each other in their haste, and just as the last got out
and locked the door the bottle burst, and out came the
dragon, very fiery, and swelling more and more every
minute, and he began to eat the sacks of gold, and crunch
up the pearls and diamonds and rubies as you do "hundreds and thousands".

By breakfast-time he had devoured the whole of the
Prince's treasures, and when the Prince came along the
street at about eleven, he met the dragon coming out of the
broken door of the treasury, with molten gold still dripping from his jaws. Then the Prince turned and ran for his

life, and as he ran towards the dragon-proof tower the little white Princess saw him coming, and she ran down and unlocked the door and let him in, and slammed the dragon-proof door in the fiery face of the dragon, who sat down and whined outside, because he wanted the Prince very much indeed.

The Princess took Prince Tiresome into the best room, and laid the cloth, and gave him cream and eggs and white grapes, and honey and bread, with many other things, yellow and white and good to eat, and she served him just as kindly as she would have done if he had been any-one else instead of the bad Prince who had taken away her kingdom and kept it for himself—because she was a true Princess and had a heart of gold.

When he had eaten and drunk he begged the Princess to show him how to lock and unlock the door, and the nurse was asleep, so there was no one to tell the Princess not to, and she did.

"You turn the key like this," she said, "and the door keeps shut. But turn it nine times round the wrong way, and the door flies open."

And so it did. And the moment it opened the Prince pushed the white Princess out of her tower, just as he had pushed her out of her kingdom, and shut the door. For he wanted to have the tower all for himself. And there she was in the street, and on the other side of the way the dragon was sitting whining, but he did not try to eat her, because—though the old nurse did not know it—dragons cannot eat white Princesses with hearts of gold.

The Princess could not walk through the streets of the town in her milky-silky gown with the daisies on it, and with no hat and no gloves, so she turned the other way, and ran out across the meadows, towards the wood. She had never been out of her tower before, and the soft grass under her feet felt like grass of Paradise.

She ran right into the thickest part of the wood, because she did not know what her heart was made of, and she was afraid of the dragon, and there in a dell she came on Elfinn and his five-and-seventy fine pigs. He was playing his flute, and around him the pigs were dancing cheerfully on their hind legs.

"Oh dear," said the Princess, "do take care of me. I am so frightened."

"I will," said Elfinn, putting his arms round her. "Now you are quite safe. What were you frightened of?"

"The dragon," she said.

"So it's got out of the silver bottle," said Elfinn. "I hope it's eaten the Prince."

"No," said Sabrinetta, "but why?"

So he told her of the mean trick that the Prince had played him.

"And he promised me half his kingdom and the hand of his cousin the Princess," said Elfinn.

"Oh dear, what a shame!" said Sabrinetta, trying to get out of his arms. "How dared he?"

"What's the matter?" he asked, holding her tighter; "it *was* a shame, or at least I thought so. But *now* he may keep his kingdom, half and whole, if I may keep what I have."

"What's that?" asked the Princess.

"Why, you—my pretty, my dear," said Elfinn, "and as for the Princess, his cousin—forgive me, dearest heart, but when I asked for her I hadn't seen the real Princess, the only Princess, *my* Princess."

"Do you mean me?" said Sabrinetta.

"Who else?" he asked.

"Yes, but five minutes ago you hadn't seen me!"

"Five minutes ago I was a pig-keeper—now I've held you in my arms I'm a Prince, though I should have to keep pigs to the end of my days."

"But you haven't asked *me?*" said the Princess.

"*You* asked *me* to take care of you," said Elfinn, "and I will—all my life long."

So that was settled, and they began to talk of really important things, such as the dragon and the Prince, and all the time Elfinn did not know that this was the Princess, but he knew that she had a heart of gold: and he told her so, many times.

"The mistake," said Elfinn, "was in not having a dragon-proof bottle. I see that now."

"Oh, is that all?" said the Princess. "I can easily get you one of those—because everything in my tower is dragon proof. We ought to do something to settle the dragon and save the little children."

So she started off to get the bottle, and she would not let Elfinn come with her.

"If what you say is true," she said—"if you are sure that I have a heart of gold, the dragon won't hurt me, and somebody *must* stay with the pigs."

Elfinn was quite sure, so he let her go.

She found the door of her tower open. The dragon had waited patiently for the Prince, and the moment he opened the door and came out, though he was only out for an instant to post a letter to his Prime Minister, saying where he was, and asking them to send the fire brigade to deal with the fiery dragon, the dragon ate him. Then the dragon went back to the wood, because it was getting near his time to grow small for the night.

So Sabrinetta went in and kissed her nurse, and made her a cup of tea and explained what was going to happen, and that she had a heart of gold, so the dragon couldn't eat her; and the nurse saw that, of course, the Princess was quite safe, and kissed her and let her go.

She took the dragon-proof bottle, made of burnished brass, and ran back to the wood, and to the dell where Elfinn was sitting among his sleek black pigs, waiting for her.

"I thought you were never coming back," he said; "you have been away a year, at least."

The Princess sat down beside him among the pigs, and they held each other's hands till it was dark, and then the dragon came crawling over the moss, scorching it as he came, and getting smaller as he crawled, and curled up under the root of the tree.

"Now then," said Elfinn, "you hold the bottle,"—then

he poked and prodded the dragon with bits of stick till it crawled into the dragon-proof bottle. But there was no stopper.

"Never mind," said Elfinn, "I'll put my finger in for a stopper."

"No, let me," said the Princess; but, of course, Elfinn would not let her. He stuffed his finger into the top of the bottle, and the Princess cried out:

"The sea—the sea—run for the cliffs!" And off they went, with the five-and-seventy pigs trotting steadily after them in a long, black procession.

The bottle got hotter and hotter in Elfinn's hands, because the dragon inside was puffing fire and smoke with all his might. Hotter, and hotter, and hotter, but Elfinn held on till they came to the cliff-edge, and there was the dark blue sea, and the whirlpool going round and round.

Elfinn lifted the bottle high above his head and hurled it out between the stars and the sea, and it fell in the middle of the whirlpool.

"We've saved the country," said the Princess. "You've saved the little children. Give me your hands."

"I can't," said Elfinn; "I shall never be able to take your dear hands again. My hands are burnt off."

And so they were: there were only black cinders where his hands ought to have been. The Princess kissed them, and cried over them, and tore pieces of her silky-milky gown to tie them up with, and the two went back to the tower and told the nurse all about everything. And the pigs sat outside and waited.

"He is the bravest man in the world," said Sabrinetta. "He has saved the country and the little children; but, oh, his hands—his poor, dear, darling hands!"

Here the door of the room opened, and the oldest of the

five-and-seventy pigs came in. It went up to Elfinn and rubbed itself against him with little, loving grunts.

"See the dear creature," said the nurse, wiping away a tear; "it knows, it knows!"

Sabrinetta stroked the pig, because Elfinn had no hands for stroking or for anything else.

"The only cure for a dragon burn," said the old nurse, "is pig's fat, and well that faithful creature knows it—"

"I wouldn't for a kingdom," cried Elfinn, stroking the pig as best he could with his elbow.

"Is there no other cure?" asked the Princess.

Here another pig put its black nose in at the door, and then another and another, till the room was full of pigs, a surging mass of rounded blackness, pushing and struggling to get at Elfinn, and grunting softly in the language of true affection.

"There is *one* other," said the nurse; "the dear, affectionate beasts—they all want to die for you."

"What *is* the other cure?" said Sabrinetta, anxiously.

"If a man is burnt by a dragon," said the nurse, "and a certain number of people are willing to die for him, it is enough if each should kiss the burn, and wish it well in the depths of his loving heart."

"The number! The number!" cried Sabrinetta.

"Seventy-seven," said the nurse.

"We have only seventy-five pigs," said the Princess, "and with me that's seventy-six!"

"It must be seventy-seven—and I really *can't* die for him, so nothing can be done," said the nurse, sadly. "He must have cork hands."

"I knew about the seventy-seven loving people," said Elfinn. "But I never thought my dear pigs loved me so much as all this, and my dear, too—And of course, that only makes it more impossible. There's *one* other charm that cures dragon burns, though; but I'd rather be burnt black all over than marry anyone but you, my dear, my pretty."

"Why, who must you marry to cure your dragon burns?" asked Sabrinetta.

"A Princess. That's how St. George cured *his* burns."

"There now! Think of that!" said the nurse. "And I never heard tell of that cure, old as I am."

But Sabrinetta threw her arms round Elfinn's neck, and held him as though she would never let him go.

"Then it's all right, my dear, brave, precious Elfinn," she cried, "for I *am* a Princess, and you shall be my Prince. Come along, nurse—don't wait to put on your bonnet. We'll go and be married this very moment."

So they went, and the pigs came after, moving in stately blackness, two by two. And, the minute he was married to the Princess, Elfinn's hands got quite well. And the people, who were weary of Prince Tiresome and his hippopotamuses, hailed Sabrinetta and her husband as rightful Sovereigns of the land.

Next morning the Prince and Princess went out to see if the dragon had been washed ashore. They could see nothing of him; but when they looked out towards the whirlpool they saw a cloud of steam; and the fishermen reported that the water for miles round was hot enough to shave with! And as the water is hot there to this day, we may feel pretty sure that the fierceness of that dragon was such that all the waters of all the sea were not enough to cool him. The whirlpool is too strong for him to be able to get out of it, so there he spins round and round for ever and ever, doing some useful work at last, and warming the water for poor fisher-folk to shave with.

The Prince and Princess rule the land well and wisely. The nurse lives with them, and does nothing but fine sewing, and only that when she wants to very much. The Prince keeps no hippopotamuses, and is consequently very popular. The five-and-seventy devoted pigs live in white marble sties with brass knockers and "Pig" on the door-plate, and are washed twice a day with Turkish sponges and soap scented with violets, and no one objects to *their* following the Prince when he walks abroad, for they behave beautifully, and always keep to the footpath, and obey the notices about not walking on the grass. The Princess feeds them every day with her own hands, and her first edict on coming to the throne was that the word "Pork" should never be uttered on pain of death, and should, besides, be scratched out of all the dictionaries.

The Dragon at Hide-and-Seek

G. K. CHESTERTON

ONCE upon a time there was a knight who was an outlaw, that is a man hiding from the king and everybody else; and one who lived so wild and lawless a life, in being hunted from one hiding-place to another, that he had great difficulty in going to church every Sunday. Although his ordinary way of life was full of fighting, and burning, and breaking down doors, and therefore looked a little careless, he had been very carefully brought up, and it was obviously a very serious thing that he should be late for church. But he was so clever and daring in his way of getting from one place to another without being caught, that he generally managed it somehow. And it was often a considerable disturbance to the congregation when he came with a great crash flying in through the big stained-glass window and smashing it to atoms, having been patiently hanging on a gargoyle outside for half an hour; or, when he dropped suddenly out of the belfry, where he had been hiding in one of the big bells, and alighted almost on the heads of the worshippers. Nor were they better pleased when he preferred to dig a hole in the churchyard and crawl under the church-wall, coming up suddenly under a lifted paving-stone in the middle of the nave or the chancel. They were too well-behaved, of course, to notice the incident during the service; and the

204

more just among them admitted that even outlaws must
get to church somehow; but it caused a certain amount of
talk in the town, and the history of the knight and his
wonderful way of hiding everywhere and anywhere was
by this time familiar to the whole countryside. At last this
knight, who was called Sir Laverok, began to feel so sure
of his power of escaping and hiding, whenever he wanted
to, that he would come into the market-place in the most
impudent manner when any great business was being
transacted, such as the elections of the guilds, or even to
the coronation of the King, to whom he addressed some
well-chosen words of advice about his public duties, in a
loud voice from the chimney-pot of an adjoining house.
Often, when the King and his lords were out hunting, or
even when they were in camp during a great war, they
would look up and see Sir Laverok perched like a bird on a
tree above their heads, and ever ready with friendly coun-
sels and almost fatherly good wishes. But though they
pursued him with emotions of uninterrupted rage, lasting
over several months, they were never able to discover
what were the holes and corners in which he hid himself.
They were forced to admit that his talent for disappearing
into undiscovered places was of the highest order, and that
in a children's game of Hide-and-Seek he would have
covered himself with ever-lasting glory; but they all felt
that a fugitive from justice should be strictly forbidden to
cultivate genius of this kind.

Now it was just about this time that there fell upon the
whole of that country an enormous calamity far worse than
any war or pestilence. It was of a kind which we have very
few chances of experiencing nowadays; though in the
other matter of wars and diseases our opportunities are
still wide and varied. There had appeared in the wilderness

to the north of that country, a monster of huge size and horrible habits and disposition; a monster who might have been called for the sake of simplicity, a dragon, only he had feet like an elephant, but a hundred times bigger, with which he used to stamp and crush everything to a flat and fine paste before he licked it up with a tongue as long and large as the Great Sea Serpent; and his great jaws opened wide like a whale's, only that they could have swallowed a shoal of whales as if they were whitebait. No weapons or missiles seemed to be of any avail against him; for his skin was plated with iron of incredible thickness. Indeed, some declared that he was entirely composed of iron, and that he had been made out of that material by a magician who lived beyond the wilderness, where such crafts and spells were more seriously studied. Indeed, it was hinted by some that the land of the magicians was in every way in advance of their own, and well worthy of emulation; and that if anyone objected that this marvellous machinery had no apparent effect except in killing people and destroying beautiful things, he should be rebuked as one lacking in enterprise and a larger outlook upon the future. But those who said this, commonly said it before they had actually met the new animal; and it was noticed that after meeting him they seldom uttered these thoughts, or, indeed, any other.

The monster may have been made of iron, and his nerves and muscles may have been, as some said, made like an arrangement of wheels and wires, but he was most unmistakably alive; and proved it by having a hearty appetite and an evident enjoyment of life. He trampled and devoured first, all the fortifications of the frontier, and then the castles and the larger towns of the interior; and by the time that he was marching towards the capital, the

King and his courtiers were all climbing to the tops of towers, and everybody else to the tops of trees. These precautions proved inadequate in practical experience; in very practical experience. So long as the monster could be seen twenty miles away like a marching mountain, already fantastic in outline, but still blue or purple with distance, and there was no other sign of him except a slight shaking of the houses as in a mild earthquake, these conjectures and expedients could be debated copiously, if not always calmly. But when the creature came near enough for his habits to be closely studied, it was clear that he could tread down trees like grass, and flatten out castles like houses of cards. It became more and more the fashion to seek out less showy and more secluded country resorts; the whole population, led by magistrates, merchants, and all its natural leaders, fleeing with startling rapidity to the mountains and concealing themselves in holes and caverns, which they blocked behind them with big rocks. Even this was not very successful; the monster proceeded to scale the mountains with the gaiety of a goat, to kick the rocky barricades to pieces, letting in daylight on the cowering company within; and many of them were able to recognize the familiar shape of the long and curling tongue of the intelligent creature, exploring their retreat and coiling and twisting and darting about in a very playful and sportive manner. Those who had not found any hole to crawl into, and who were clinging in crowds to the crags higher up the hill, were at this moment, however, surprised with a start that almost took their thoughts for an instant off the universal peril. On the highest crag of all, above their heads had appeared suddenly the figure of Sir Laverok with his old spear in his hand, with his sword girt around his ragged armour, and the wind waving about his wild hair

that was the colour of flame. In all that huddling crowd it
was only the man in hiding who stood out conspicuous;
and only the man fleeing from justice who did not flee.

"I am not afraid," he said in answer to their wild cries.
"You know I have a trick of finding my way to places of
safety. And as it happens, I know a castle to which I shall
retreat, and to which the dragon can never come."

"But my good Sir," said the Chancellor, pausing in the
act of trying to creep into a rabbit-burrow, "the dragon
can grind castles to powder with his heel. I regret to say
that he showed not the least embarrassment even in
approaching the Law Courts."

"I know of a castle which he cannot reach," said Sir
Laverok.

"The offensive animal," said the Lord Chamberlain,
poking his head for a moment out of a hole in the ground,
"actually entered the King's private chamber without
knocking."

"I know of a private chamber that he cannot enter,"
replied the outlaw knight.

"It is very doubtful," came the muffled voice of the Lord
High Admiral from somewhere underground, "whether
we shall even be safe in any of the caverns."

"I know a cavern where I shall be safe," said Sir
Laverok.

At the foot of the steep slope to which they clung spread
a large plateau like a plain; and over this bare tableland, at
the moment, the monster was prowling up and down like
a polar bear, considering what he would destroy next.
Every time he turned his head towards them, the crowds
clambered a little higher up the hill; but they soon saw, to
their astonishment, that Sir Laverok was not climbing up,
but climbing down. He dropped from the last overhanging

rock, and rushed out upon the plain against the monster; when he came within a short distance, the knight gave one wild leap and threw his spear like a thunderbolt.

What happened in the flash of that thunderbolt nobody in the crowd seemed to know. Those who knew them best were of opinion that they all shut their eyes tight, and most probably fell flat on their faces. Others say that the monster stamped his foot upon his enemy with so stunning a shock that a cloud of dust rolled up to the clouds of heaven, and for a moment hid the whole scene. Others, again, explained that the vast immeasurable bulk of the monster had come between them and the victim. Anyhow, it is certain that when that vast bulk turned once more and began swaying and lurching backwards and forwards on its lonely prowl, no sign of the victim could be seen. Probably he had been stamped to mire as everything else had been. But if it were conceivable that he had indeed escaped, as he had boasted, it was hard to say where; as there did not seem to be anywhere for him to escape to. And the authorities in the holes and caves could not but regret that they had not condemned him to be burned as a wizard instead of hanged as a rebel, whenever they should have put the final touch of the sentence by carrying it into effect. They comforted themselves in the cave by the reflection that at least no hasty capture or premature execution had yet put it out of their power to rectify the mistake; but for the moment it seemed clear that their chances either of hanging or burning the gentleman were further off than ever.

Just at that moment, however, there was a new interruption. It so happened that the King's third daughter was standing in the crowd on the slope; for all the elder members of the royal family were enjoying a temporary and semi-official retirement from the cares of state at the bottom of a dry well on the other side of the mountain range. But she had been unable or unwilling to travel with the extreme rapidity which they had had the presence of mind to exhibit; for she was rather an absent-minded person, wholly without aptitude for practical politics. She was called the Princess Philomel, and was a dreamy sort of person, with long hair and blue eyes that were like the blue of distant horizons, and she was commonly very silent; but she had watched the adventure of the vanishing outlaw with more interest than she commonly showed in anything; and she startled everybody at this stage by breaking her silence and calling out in a clear voice: "Yes; he has found his fairy castle where no dragon can come."

The more dignified Councillors of State were just venturing to put their noses above ground in order to remonstrate respectfully against the breach of etiquette, when everybody's attention was again distracted to the monster, who was behaving in an even more extraordinary way than usual. Instead of pacing backwards and forwards with a certain pomposity as he had done before, he was bounding to and fro, taking totally unnecessary leaps into the air and clawing in a most uncomfortable and inconsequent fashion.

"What is the matter with him now?" enquired the Master of the Buckhounds, who was something of a student of animal life, and would, under other circumstances, have been much interested in the phenomenon.

"The monster is angry," replied the Princess Philomel in the same absolute if abstracted fashion. "He is angry because the knight has reached the magic chamber and cannot be found."

If the monster was indeed exhibiting anger, it would

seem that his anger had an element of self-reproach. For he was evidently clawing and scratching at himself rather in the manner of a dog hunting a flea, but much more savagely.

"Can he be killing himself?" asked the Lord Chancellor hopefully. "I am the keeper of the King's conscience, and not, of course, the keeper of the dragon's. But it seems possible that his conscience, if once aroused, would find in retrospect some legitimate ground for remorse."

"Nonsense," said the Chamberlain, "why should he kill himself?"

"If it comes to that," answered the other, "why should he fight himself, as he seems to be doing?"

"Because," answered the Princess, "Sir Laverok has at last reached the cavern where he is safe."

But even as she spoke, a further and final change seemed to pass over the monster. For a moment it looked as if he had turned into two or three different monsters, for the different parts of him were behaving in different ways. One hind leg rested as calmly on the earth as the column of a temple, while the other was kicking wildly up behind and thrashing the air like the sail of a windmill. One eye was standing out of the head in hideous prominence, and rolling round and round like a catherine-wheel of fury, while the other was already closed with the placid expression of a cow who had gone to sleep. Then the next moment both eyes were closed, and both feet stationary, and the whole monster, with a deprecating expression, turned his back and began to retreat towards the plains at an amiable and ambling trot.

Thus began the last phase of the celebrated Dragon of the Wilderness, which was more of a mystery than his wildest massacres and deeds of destruction. He interfered

with nobody; he stood politely on one side for people to
pass; he even succeeded, with some signs of reluctance, in
becoming a vegetarian and subsisting entirely upon grass.
But when the ultimate goal of his pilgrimage was discovered, the surprise was even more general. The wondering and still doubtful crowds that followed him across
that country became gradually convinced of the incredible
idea that he intended to go to church. Moreover, he
approached the sacred edifice in a far more tactful and
unobtrusive and respectful way than Sir Laverok had done
in the old days, when he broke windows and tore up pave-
ments in his indiscriminating excess of punctuality. Finally,
the monster surprised them most of all by kneeling down
and opening his mouth very wide with an ingratiating
expression; and the Princess surprised them still more by
walking inside.

Something in the way in which she did it revealed to the
more thoughtful among them the fact that Sir Laverok
had been inside the animal all the time. It is unnecessary to
repeat here the explanations which gradually enlightened
them about the inner truth of the story or the inner
machinery of the dragon. This exact and scientific narrative is also addressed only to the thoughtful. And these
will have no difficulty in guessing that a magnificent
marriage ceremony took place in the interior of the dragon
which was treated as a temporary chapel while within the
precincts of the consecrated building. They may even form
some notion of what was meant when the Princess, who
was given to oracular remarks, said, "The whole world
will behave differently when heroes find their hiding-place
in the world." But it must be confessed that those learned
men, the Chancellor and the Chamberlain, could make
very little of it.

Conrad and the Dragon

L. P. HARTLEY

ONCE upon a time there was a boy who lived with his mother and father in a country five days' journey beyond the boundaries of Europe. As he was only twelve years old when this story begins, he did not have to work for his living, but played about in the woods. Sometimes he would stand and watch his two brothers felling trees and sawing them up, for, like his father, they were foresters, and every now and then they would let him ride home astride a tree-trunk, jogging up and down above the horses. This he enjoyed, when once he got over the fear of falling off, and he would have joined them oftener, but he was afraid lest his elder brother Leo might say: "Now, Conrad, it's your turn to do something; just mind those horses for ten minutes," or: "Conrad, come here and lean your heavy weight against the sapling, so that I can get the axe to it." Then Conrad would have to go, unless his other brother Rudolph chimed in with: "Oh, let the boy alone, Leo; he's more hindrance than help." Then Conrad would be half glad and half sorry. He wanted to lend a hand, but he was afraid the horse might tread on his toes, or the sapling spring up and hit him. He was very fond of his brothers, especially the younger, Rudolph, and he admired them. They were so strong and capable. He did not believe he would ever be able to do what they did, even when he grew up. "I am not meant to be a forester," he said to himself.

One afternoon Leo put the axe in his hands and tried more persistently than ever to teach him how to use it. Conrad had been only half-attending; he swung the axe clumsily, and it glanced off the tree on to his foot, making a deep gash in his boot. Leo spoke sharply to him for his awkwardness, and Conrad, without waiting to hear what Rudolph might say in his defence, dropped the axe and ran away, crying; nor did he pause for breath until the noise that came from the clearing had ceased altogether.

Here the forest was very thick and silent, and though there seemed to be plenty of little paths going hither and thither, a stranger to the wood would have found that they led nowhere in particular; to an abandoned clearing, perhaps, or just into undergrowth. But Conrad, who knew this part of the wood by heart, was not at all alarmed. He was feeling too hurt and angry with his brothers to be sorry that he had damaged his boot; what he dreaded was that the axe might have cut his foot, in which case he would have to swallow his pride, and go back to his brothers to beg a ride; for he was a long way from home.

He examined the gash, but there was no sign of blood; and when he took off his boot to look closer he found that the stocking was slightly cut, but the skin below it was unharmed. What a lucky escape! It must be magic, Conrad thought—white magic, much rarer than the black kind which he had been warned against, and which was all too common in this part of the world. How nice if he could meet, in some dell or coppice, the good fairy who, at the critical moment, had turned the axe's edge! He peered about; he kissed the air, hoping to attract her; but if she was there she remained invisible. But Conrad, encouraged by the discovery that he was unhurt, felt twice the boy he was. So far from running back to his brothers, he would prove to them that he did not need their protection. He would press on through the forest farther than he had ever gone before, and would not be home till nightfall. He had some food in his satchel, and, as it was early autumn, there were plenty of berries on the trees. He started off.

Soon the wood changed its character. Instead of being flat, it grew hilly, a succession of narrow valleys which Conrad always seemed to have to cross at their deepest point, scrambling up and down as best he could, for path there was none. He began to feel tired, and the sharp hard leather of his damaged boot stuck into him and hurt him. He kept on meaning to turn back, but whenever he reached the crest of a ridge it looked such a little way to the next that he always decided to cross just one more valley. They were long and empty, lit up their whole length by the sun which, away on Conrad's right, was now so low that he could see it without lifting his eyes. It would soon be night. Suddenly he lost heart and made up his mind to stop at the next hill-top. It was only a few yards' climb.

But once there, what a sight met his eyes—worth the whole journey, worth far, far more than all the efforts he had made. An immense valley, like the others only larger, and flooded with orange light, stretched away to the left; and blocking the end a huge square rock, almost a mountain, with a castle built into its summit, so cunningly you could not tell where rock ended and stone began. Conrad strained his eyes. In the clear air of that country, of course, it was possible to see an immense distance; the castle might be five miles away, might be ten, might be twenty.

But there was a picture of it in the kitchen at home, and he recognized it at once. It was the royal castle, the palace of the King.

Clearly something very exciting was happening. The castle was gaily decorated with flags; bright-coloured rugs and tapestries hung from the windows, and scarlet streamers attached to the pinnacles flapped and floated in the breeze. In front of the castle was a huge black mass, divided by a white road; this mass Conrad presently made out to be a great crowd of people ranged on either side of the highway; soldiers on horseback were keeping the road clear, while along it in fours marched heralds blowing trumpets, and moving so slowly they scarcely seemed to move at all.

All at once the trumpeters halted, turned, stepped back and lined the road, their trumpets still extended. There was a pause in which nothing seemed to move; the breeze held its breath, the flags, hanging straight down, looked little thicker than their poles. Then in the mouth of the long white channel appeared four men on horseback, followed at some distance by a single horseman, whose uniform glittered as though with jewels, and on whose helmet was a great white plume. His head was slightly bent; whether in pride or humility, Conrad could not tell; perhaps he was acknowledging the cheers of the spectators, who had broken into frenzied movement, waving their arms and flinging their hats into the air.

So the single horseman proceeded, until the whole crowd, and Conrad with it, had stared their fill at him, and the first flight of steps seemed only a few yards away. Exactly what happened then Conrad never remembered. There was a movement in the face of the living rock, a wrinkling and crumbling, and a drift of powdery smoke

flung up into the air. A hole appeared in the hillside, and out of it came a head—a snake-like head, blacker than the hole it issued from, solid as ebony, large as the shadow of a cloud. It writhed this way and that on its round, thick neck, then suddenly darted forward. The crowd gave way on either hand, leaving in the centre a bulging space like an egg. Conrad saw the plumed horseman look back over his shoulder. That way lay safety; but he preferred not to save himself. Conrad did not wait to see him ride to his death; his last impression of the scene before he took to his heels was of a sudden hurricane that caught the face of the castle and stripped it bare of every flag, carpet and tapestry that emblazoned it.

Ill news travels fast, and thus it was that when night fell Conrad's absence from home was scarcely noticed. "What can have happened to the boy?" his mother asked more than once; but nobody took the matter up; they were too busy, the brother and their friends, discussing the awful fate that had overtaken Princess Hermione's suitor. The Princess was to have been betrothed that day to the heir of a neighbouring monarch. He was a handsome young man —gallant and brave—an excellent match in every way.

"Had the Princess ever seen him?" asked Conrad's mother.

"How does that affect the matter?" exclaimed her husband. "The alliance would have made us the strongest nation upon earth. Who will want to marry her now?"

"There will be plenty," said Leo promptly. "The Princess is but seventeen, and the most beautiful woman in the world."

Nobody denied this, for it was known to be true. The Princess's beauty was so great it had already become a proverb. The men of other countries, when they wanted to describe a beautiful women, said she was as lovely as a rose, or as the day, or as a star; but the people of this country, if they wanted to praise something, said it was as beautiful as Princess Hermione. She was so beautiful that anything she did, even speaking, made her less lovely, ruffled her beauty as it were; so she did little and spoke seldom. Also she rarely went about in public; it was unfair to people; they could not help falling in love with her. So retiring was her nature that ordinary folk like Conrad and his brothers knew little about her except that she was lovely.

"Of course," said Leo, "some one will have to go properly armed to fight this dragon. That poor fellow didn't have a chance in his fine clothes. The King may call out the Militia; or perhaps they'll just stop its hole up and starve it out."

"I'm afraid it will be a great shock to the Princess," their mother said.

Thereupon they fell to arguing as to where the Princess could have been when the Dragon burst out from the cliff and devoured her luckless suitor. One said she had been seen at a window; another that she was praying in the chapel. Of course it was all hearsay. At last their father, tired of the argument, observed.

"I don't suppose she was anywhere in particular."

"Why, she must have been somewhere," they protested.

"Well, I've told you what I think," said he; and at that moment Conrad came in.

He expected a beating for being so late, and at any other time he might have got it. But tonight, so great was the excitement, his tardy arrival was treated as something of a joke. To turn their attention away from his lateness he meant to tell them at once the story of what he had seen in the wood—he had got it by heart. But no sooner had he begun than, partly from exhaustion, but more from sickness as the details came up before his mind, he turned faint and had to stop. His brothers laughed at him, and returned to their own pet theories of what had happened at the castle. Conrad felt disappointed. Though coming home had taken him twice as long as going, it had all been a marvellous adventure, which he thought his parents and brothers would clamour to hear about! Whereas Leo hardly took any interest in his story, and even Rudolph said that from such a position he couldn't have seen anything with certainty. Just because they were grown up they did not believe his experiences could matter to anyone. They went on discussing how many people beside the Prince the Dragon had eaten, and what had happened to the torrent of black blood it was supposed to have emitted—things they knew nothing about. What a tame ending to an exciting day!

Of course, the court went into mourning, and a general fast was proclaimed, for it was rightly decided to neglect nothing that might lead to the Dragon's destruction. But from the first the Prince's would-be avengers were faced by an almost insuperable obstacle. The Dragon had utterly disappeared, leaving no trace; even the hole by which it came out had closed up; and professional mountaineers tied to ropes searched the face of the rock with pickaxes, and even microscopes, to find an opening, without success. The very wallflowers that the Princess was reported to be so fond of bloomed there just as before; and popular opinion became irritated against the experts who, it said, were looking in the wrong place, and deliberately pro-longing their job. Short of blasting the rock, which would have endangered the castle, every means was tried to make the Dragon come out. A herald was sent, quaking with fright, to ask it to state its terms; because those learned in Dragonology declared that in the past dragons had been appeased by an annual sacrifice of men and maidens. When the Dragon made no reply the herald was instructed to play upon its vanity, and issue a formal challenge on behalf of one or other of the most redoubtable champions in the country. Let it name a day and settle the matter by single combat. Still the Dragon made no sign, and the herald, emboldened by this display of cowardice, said that since it was such a poor-spirited thing he was ready to fight it himself, or get his little brother to do so. But the Dragon took no notice at all.

As the weeks lengthened into months without any demonstration by the Dragon, public confidence grew apace. One circumstance especially fostered this. It was feared that the neighbouring monarch who had so un-luckily lost his eldest son would demand compensation, possibly with threats. But his attitude proved unexpectedly conciliatory. He absolved them from all negligence, he said; no one could be forearmed against a Dragon; and his son had met a gallant death on behalf (as it were) of the most beautiful lady in the world. After this handsome declaration it was hoped that he himself must come forward as a candidate for the Princess Hermione's hand, for he was a widower. But he did not.

Suitors were not lacking, however; indeed, since the appearance of the Dragon they had multiplied enormously. The fame of that event went abroad, carrying the Princess's name into remote countries where even the rumour of her beauty had failed to penetrate. Now she was not only beautiful, she was unfortunate: the Dragon, some said, was the price she had paid for her beauty. All this, combined with the secrecy which made her way of life a matter of speculation, invested the Princess with an extraordinary glamour. Everyone in the land, even the humblest, wanted to do something for her, they knew not what. Daily she received sackfuls of letters, all telling the same tale: that she was the most wonderful of women, that the writer adored her and wished that he, not the Prince, had had the honour of dying for her. A few even expressed the hope that the Dragon would re-appear, so that they might put their devotion to the test.

But of course no one believed that it really would. Some who had not been eye-witnesses declared that the Dragon was an hallucination; that the Prince had just died of joy upon finding himself at last so near the Princess, and that the spectators, drunk with excitement, had imagined the rest. The majority felt confident for a different reason. Dragons, like comets and earthquakes, were things of rare occurrence. We know little about them, they argued, but at any rate we can be sure of this: if we have seen *one* Dragon in our lives, we are not likely to see another. Many carried this argument a step further, and maintained that the kingdom had never been so safe from visitation by Dragons as it was now; it had got the Dragon over, so to speak.

Before eighteen months were up the Dragon had passed into a joke. In effigy it was dragged round at fairs and processions, and made to perform laughable antics. Writers in the newspapers, when they wanted to describe a ground-less fear or a blessing in disguise, referred to it as "Princess Hermione's Dragon." Such as gave the monster serious thought congratulated themselves that it had come and gone without doing them any personal harm. Factories sprang up and business flourished, and in the tide of national prosperity, a decent period having elapsed, another suitor presented himself for the honour of winning Princess Hermione's hand.

He came of a royal house scarcely less distinguished (the newspapers said more distinguished) than his predecessor's. Preparations for his reception were made on a grander scale than before, and they were made on a completely different plan, so that there might be no question of com-parison with the former ceremony. One alteration was this: a detachment of machine-gunners, armed with a new type of gun and carrying many rounds of blank ammuni-tion, was posted on a convenient ledge commanding the spot where the Dragon had broken out. And there was to be one further change. The Princess's first suitor, when he realized his danger and turned to face the Dragon, had cried out "Dearest Hermione " or something to that effect, some protestation of loyalty and love; he had not time to say much and nobody could recollect his exact words. The new suitor proposed that he should kneel at the foot of the steps and make a little speech, half a prayer, half a declaration of love.

And so, when the day came the people assembled to enjoy the spectacle in greater numbers than before. They were in the highest spirits, for the ceremony had a double appeal: it was to celebrate the betrothal of their beloved Princess and her deliverance from the Dragon. Salvoes from the machine guns mingling with the strains of martial music raised their excitement to frenzy. The silence in which the Prince kneeled down to do homage to his bride-to-be was painful in its intensity. But no sooner had the last words passed his lips than there came a rumbling roar, a convulsion in the cliff, and the poor wretch was whirled aloft between the Dragon's jaws, to disappear in the mysterious recess of the hillside.

The scene that followed was indescribable, and for a week, throughout the length and breadth of the kingdom, panic reigned. Frantic efforts were made to explain the causes of the calamity in the wickedness of individuals or in the mismanagement of the country. Impostors appeared and won a short hour of importance by declaring that so-and-so was the culprit; and many innocent persons perished at the hands of the mob. Even the King was covertly censured.

Only the Princess escaped blame. As before, she was alone, no one knew exactly where, at the precise moment of the catastrophe; but when she was found, a few minutes later, half-swooning in her room, her courage impressed everyone. She was soon able to write with her own hand a letter of condolence to the man who had so nearly been her father-in-law. When published in the newspapers, its eloquent phrases touched all hearts. Most miserable of women, she said, she had been the means of bringing death to two brave men—the second perhaps even more promising than the first. But what raised such a fury of protest was her concluding sentence—that she thought she must retire from the world. From all quarters of the country came letters begging her not to—so numerous that special mail-trains had to run.

There was no difficulty in finding fresh champions for the Princess; her fame had increased with her misfortunes. She had never been so popular. Public confidence was reinvigorated by the verdict of military experts, who asserted that the disaster could not have happened if the machine gunners had been properly armed. "Give it a few rounds rapid," they said, "and we shan't be troubled by it any more." The populace believed them. There had been too much muddling along; preparations for the Princess's coming betrothal must be put in the hands of the military. The Commander-in-chief announced that no member of the general public would be admitted to the ceremony, for the Dragon, though its days were now numbered, was still not to be trifled with. The new Prince's escort (he had already been chosen) was to be formed exclusively of picked troops, drilled to perfection and armed with the latest weapons. As they marched along the valley to take up their positions the sun shone down on thousands of steel helmets. They looked invincible.

Alas! alas! The Prince had no sooner voiced his passionate plea than the hillside quaked and the Dragon darted out. It was warmly welcomed. Ten thousand soft-nosed rifle bullets must have struck it, and volleys of machine-gun fire, but in vain. The cruel eyes never even blinked. One satisfaction it missed, however. The firing continued long after the Prince was in mid-air. He must have been riddled with bullets, stone-dead, before the Dragon got him into its lair. He had been killed by his own defenders, a possibility that had never entered into the calculations of the military authorities.

To chronicle the events of the next two years is a grievous task, and one that the historian would gladly skip. The country went through a miserable time. The supply of eligible Princes would not last for ever, so it was decided to accept the offers of champions who, though of good birth, were more remarkable for valour than for rank. Supposing it did not fall to the spear of the first, seven different warriors were to engage the Dragon on seven successive days. If it survived these encounters, it would at any rate be tired, and in no fit state to engage the Prince of royal blood, though of no great personal prowess, who was to attempt it on the eighth day. But the Dragon was not exhausted at all; it seemed to have profited from practice, and found the Royal Prince as easy a prey as his seven predecessors.

So ended the first phase. The country's nobility shed its blood in gallons, and still volunteers pressed forward, drawn from its thinning ranks. But then began an agitation, founded partly on democratic feeling, partly on the devotion which every man in the country worthy of the name, aye, and many outside it, cherished for the Princess Hermione: Why should the glory of her rescue be confined to a privileged class? The King gave his consent; the Chamberlain's office was nearly stampeded; and at last a blacksmith, a redoubtable fellow, was selected as the People's Champion against the Dragon.

Of course there was no thought of his marrying the Princess, nor did he presume to such an honour. As he stood at the foot of the steps, accompanied only by a handful of friends, who came at their own risk (the public had long since been excluded), he would gladly have allayed his nervousness by saying a few words, if not of love to the Princess, at least of defiance to the Dragon. But he was not allowed to speak; and this, much as he resented it at the time, undoubtedly saved his life; for the Dragon did not condescend to appear.

No, its hate, rage, and lust of blood were clearly reserved for those who really loved the Princess and were in a position to marry her. The Dragon was not the enemy of the people, but the enemy of the Princess.

As soon as this was realized there was obviously only one thing to do, and the King gave his consent to it, though sorely against his will. Anyone, of whatever station in life, who could kill the Dragon should marry the Princess and have half the kingdom as well.

As always, when a last desperate step is taken, hope surged up to greet the new proposal. It was obviously the right solution; why had no one thought of it before, and saved all this bloodshed? Enthusiasm ran high; combats were of almost daily occurrence; and in each one, though the upshot was always the same, the newspapers (seeing that they ran no risk, the public was again admitted to the scene) found some encouraging circumstance: the Dragon had lost a tooth, or its inky crest was streaked with grey, or it was a second late in appearing or it was fat and slow with good living, or it had grinned and looked almost benevolent. The unfortunate heroes had displayed, this one a neat piece of foot-work; that, a shrewd thrust which might have pierced the side of a ship; while they were all commended for some original phrase, some prettily-turned compliment in their address to the Princess.

Not the least part of the whole ordeal was the framing

of this speech; it was the only way by which the competitors could measure their skill against each other, since their performances against the Dragon hardly differed at all. There was no doubt the Dragon disliked hearing the Princess praised; the more ardent and graceful the language in which she was wooed, the more vigorous was its onslaught.

Leo, Conrad's brother, was one of the first to volunteer and the Dragon gobbled him up. Conrad missed his fiery, impatient brother. Little had his parents realized that the Dragon which had seemed an affair for Kings and Queens and Governments, would take its toll from them. But their pride in their son's sacrifice upheld them, and lessened their grief. Conrad, however, grew more despondent daily. He dreaded lest Rudolph, his favourite brother, should take it into his head to challenge the Dragon. Rudolph was less hot-headed than Leo, and he was engaged to be married. Married men were forbidden to fight the Dragon—though more than one, concealing his true condition, had gone out to meet a bachelor's death.

Conrad lost no opportunity of praising the charms of Charlotte, his brother's sweetheart; in and out of season he begged Rudolph to marry her. In his anxiety for his brother's safety he more than once let drop a disparaging remark about the Princess, comparing her unfavourably to Charlotte. Rudolph told him to shut up or he would get himself into trouble.

"Of course, the Princess is beautiful," Conrad admitted; "but she is fair; you told me you only admired dark women. Promise me you will marry Charlotte before the month is out."

"How can I," asked Rudolph, "when I've no money and no home to take her to?"

Conrad knew that this was not strictly true; his brother was a gay young man, but he had some money laid by. Conrad, though he earned little, spent nothing at all.

"If you marry her a fortnight from today," he begged, "you shall have all my savings, and I will be a forester instead of going to the University."

It cost him something to say this, but Rudolph answered with his light laugh:

"Keep your money, my dear Conrad, you will want it when your turn comes to fight the Dragon."

This was not very encouraging, and Conrad began to ask himself: was there no other way of keeping Rudolph out of harm's reach? The King had offered an enormous prize to anyone who could suggest a solution to the Dragon problem, and many women, cripples, elderly men and confirmed husbands had sent in suggestions, among them that the intending suitor should visit the castle in disguise. This was turned down because, even if the man got safely in, the Dragon would still be at large. Another was that the Royal Magician should give place to one more competent. To this the Home Secretary replied that it was a bad plan to change horses in mid-stream; the Magician had a world-wide reputation; he had performed many noteworthy feats in the past, he knew the lay-out of the castle as no one else did, and he was a close friend of the Princess Hermione; it would be cruel to deprive her of his presence.

Most of the proposals, though meant helpfully, only put the authorities' backs up. One malcontent even dared to remark that at this rate the Princess would never get married. The newspapers made fun of him, and he lost his job.

"If only I could get *inside* the castle," thought Conrad,

"I might be able to do something. But I shall have to be very tactful."

He began to write, but the pen would not answer to his thoughts. It seemed to have a will of its own, which was struggling against his. Instead of the valuable suggestion he wanted to make, a message of very different import kept appearing on the paper, in broken phrases like: "my life to your service," "no better death than this." Tired of trying to control it, he let the pen run on; when it stopped he found he had written a little love-address to the Princess, very like those printed between heavy black lines (almost every day now) in the memorial columns of the newspapers. Puzzled, he threw the thing aside and applied himself to his task. Now it went better; he signed it, wrote "The Princess Hermione" on the envelope and took it to the post. It would be some days before it reached her, if it ever did; she must have so many letters to deal with.

When he got home he found Rudolph in the room. He was standing by the table, holding something in his hand.

"Ha, ha!" said he, "I've found you out."

Conrad could not imagine what he meant.

"Yes," went on Rudolph, putting his hands behind his back. "You've been deceiving me. You're in love with the Princess. You've been trying to persuade me not to fight the Dragon because you want the glory of killing it yourself."

Rudolph was laughing; but Conrad cried out in agitation:

"No, you don't understand."

"Well, listen then," said Rudolph, and he began to read Conrad's Declaration of Love to the Princess; mockingly at first, then more seriously, and finally with a break in his voice and tears in his eyes.

They were silent for a moment, then Conrad held out his hand for the paper. But Rudolph would not part with it.

"Don't be silly," Conrad pleaded. "Give it to me."

"What do you want it for?" asked Rudolph.

"I want to burn it!" cried Conrad recklessly.

"No, no!" said Rudolph, half laughing and gently pushing his brother away. "I must have it—it may come in useful—who knows?"

He went out, taking the paper with him. Conrad felt uncomfortable; somehow he guessed he had done a silly thing.

He had. Two days later Rudolph casually announced that he had sent in his name as a candidate for the privilege of freeing Princess Hermione from her tormentor and that his application had been accepted.

"It's fixed for Thursday," he remarked gaily. "Poor old Dragon."

His mother burst into tears; his father left the room and did not come back for an hour; but Conrad sat in his chair without noticing what was going on around him. At last he said:

"What about Charlotte?"

"Oh," said Rudolph airily, "she's anxious for me to go. She's not like you pretend to be. She's sorry for the Princess. 'I expected you'd want to go,' she said to me, 'I shall be waiting for you when you come back'."

"Was that all?" asked Conrad.

"Oh, she gave me her blessing."

Conrad pondered. "Did you tell her you were in love with the Princess?" he asked at length.

Rudolph hesitated. "I couldn't very well tell her that, could I? It wouldn't have been kind. Besides, I'm not really in love with the Princess, of course—that's the difficulty. It was only that speech you wrote—you know" (Conrad nodded) "made me feel I was. I shall just try to be in love with her as long as the combat lasts. If I didn't, you know, the Dragon wouldn't come out, and I should miss my chance. But," he added more cheerfully, "I shall recite your address, and that will deceive it."

"And then?"

"Oh then I shall just come back and marry Charlotte. She understands that. You can give us some of your money if you like. I won't take it all. I'm not greedy."

He went off whistling. Conrad's heart sank.

★

The Royal Castle's position on the solitary rock, defended by precipices on all sides save one, gave it so much natural strength that it was generally considered impregnable. According to common report, there were more rooms hollowed out of the rock than built of stones and mortar. Later, architects, taking advantage of this, had concentrated their efforts on giving grace and elegance to the exterior, adorning it with turrets and balconies of an aery delicacy.

The Princess Hermione had chosen for her favourite sitting-room a chamber, so deeply embedded in the rock that the light of day reached it only by an ingenious system of reflectors. Nor could you tell what the season was, for a fire burned there all the year round. There was only one way into it, by a narrow winding stair; but if report could be believed, there were several ways out—dark passages leading probably to bolt-holes in the rock. For

years no one had troubled to explore them, but they had a
fascination for the Princess, who knew them by heart and
sometimes surprised her parents by appearing suddenly
before them, apparently from nowhere.

She was sitting by the fireside, deep in a chair, and
looking at some papers, which neither the firelight nor the
twilight reflected down from above quite allowed her to
read. Suddenly a shadow fell across the page and she could
see nothing. The Princess looked up: a man was standing
in front of her, shutting out the firelight; she knew no
more than you or I how he had got there, but she was not
surprised to see him.

"Well," said the Magician, for it was he, "are you still
unsatisfied?"

The Princess turned her head, invisible to us; but the
shadow of her features started up on the wall, a shadow so
beautiful that (report said) it would not disappear when
the Princess turned again, but clung on with a life of its
own, until dissolved by the Magician.

"Yesterday, at any rate, was a success," the Princess
murmured.

"Will you read me what he said," asked the Magician.

"Give me some light," she commanded, and the room
began to fill with radiance.

The Princess turned over the papers in her lap.

"Rudolph, Rudolph," she muttered. "Here he is. Do
you really want to hear what the poor oaf says?"

"Is it like the others?"

"Exactly the same, only a particularly fine specimen."

Though she tried to make her voice sound unconcerned,
the Princess spoke with a certain relish; and her silhouette
stretched upon the wall trembled and changed and became
less pleasing. The Princess turned and noticed it.

"Oh, there's that thing at its tricks again," she sighed irritably. "Take it away."

The shadow faded.

"Well," she said, settling herself again in the depths of her chair, "here it is." Her voice, slightly mimicking the peasant's burr, was delicious to hear.

" 'Most Gracious Princess—Men have been known to pity the past and dread the future; never, it seems to me, with much reason until now. But now I say, in the past there was no Princess Hermione; in the future, in the far future, dearest angel (may you live for ever) there will be none; none to live for, none to die for. Therefore I say, Wretched Past! Miserable Future! And I bless this present hour in which Life and Death are one, one act in your service, one poem in your honour!' "

The Princess paused; then spoke in her own voice:

"Didn't he deserve eating?"

"Your Highness, he did."

"But now," she continued in a brisker tone, "I've got something different to read to you. Altogether different. In fact I've never received anything like it before."

The shadow, which, like a dog that dreads reproof but cannot bear its banishment, had stolen back to the wall, registered a tiny frown on the Princess's forehead.

For the letter was certainly an odd one. The writer admitted frankly that he was not brave, nor strong, nor skilled in arms. He was afraid of a mouse, so what could he do against a Dragon? The Princess was a lady of high intelligence; she would be the first to see the futility of such a sacrifice. She was always in his thoughts, and he longed to do some tiny service for her. He could not bear to think of her awaiting alone the issue of the combat between her champion and the Dragon. The strain must be terrible. He would count himself ever honoured if she would allow him to bear her company, even behind a screen, even outside the door, during those agonizing moments.

"What a pity I can't grant his request!" said the Princess when she had finished. "I like him. I like him for not wanting to offer up his life for me. I like him for thinking that women have other interests than watching men gratify their vanity by running into danger. I like him because he credits me with intelligence. I like him because he considers my feelings, and longs to be near me when there is no glory to be gained by it. I like him because he would study my moods and find out what I needed, and care for me all the day long, even when I was in no particular danger. I like him because he would love me without a whole population of terrified half-wits egging him on! I like him for a thousand things—I think I love him."

"Your Highness! Your Highness!" said the Magician, stirring uneasily. "Remember the terms of the spell."

"Repeat them; I have forgotten."

> "If he loves you,
>   And you love not,
> Your suitor's life's
>   Not worth a jot,"

sang the Magician cheerfully.

"That's all we need to know," sighed the Princess, who really recollected the spell perfectly. "It always happens that way, and always will. But go on."

> "If he loves you
>   And you love him,
> I cannot tell
>   What Chance may bring,"

chanted the Magician in a lower tone.

"But if the 'he' were Conrad," said the Princess teasingly, "surely you could make a guess? And now for the last condition."

The Magician's voice sank to a whisper:
"If you love him,
            And he reject you,
A thousand spells
            Will not protect you."

"Ha! Ha!" cried the Princess, rocking with laughter, so that the shadow on the wall flickered like a butterfly over a flower; "all the same I love this Conrad!"

"He's but a lad, your Highness, barely turned seventeen."

"The best age—I love him."

"He's a slothful sort, his letter shows; a dreamer, not a man."

"I love him."

"While you were reading I summoned his likeness here —he is ill favoured—has lost a front tooth."

"Regular features are my abhorrence—I love him."

"He is sandy-haired and freckled and untidy in his dress."

"Never mind, I love him."

"He is self-willed and obstinate; his parents can do nothing with him."

"I could; I love him."

"He likes insects and crawling things; his pockets are full of spiders and centipedes."

"I shall love them for his sake."

"He cares for waterfalls and flowers and distant views."

"I love him more than ever!"

"But," said the Magician, suddenly grave, "I'm not sure that he loves you."

"Ah!" cried the Princess, jubilation in her voice, "I love him most of all for that!"

There was a pause. The shadow on the wall swooned from the oppression of its beauty and slid to the floor.

"But of course he loves me," the Princess murmured to herself. "Everyone does, and so must he."

She looked up at the Magician for confirmation; but he had gone. Then she saw that something was missing.

"Magician! Magician!" she cried, "you've taken my Conrad's letter. I want it back!"

But the Magician, if he heard her, did not answer.

Conrad's suggestion, when published in the papers, produced a disagreeable impression. It was called mawkish and unmanly and insulting to the dignity of the Princess. "Forester's Son wants to be Male Nurse," ran the headline. However, the letter was so inept, it could not be taken seriously. Conrad was evidently a little weak in the head. Naturally, the Princess would have liked company in the hour of trial—and many were ready to offer it, from the King downwards; she had no need of the services of a woodman's unlicked cub. But she preferred to spare her friends the sight of her mental and physical anguish. It was the best she could do, she said in her gracious winning way, to soften the burden a miserable fate had cast, through her, upon her countrymen. So she retired and encountered her dark destiny alone, with the aid of such courage as she could summon. Conrad, the article concluded charitably, was no doubt too thick in the head to understand such delicacy of feeling; but surely his parents might have stopped him from making a fool of himself in public; the noble example of his brothers might have stopped him.

Conrad was too miserable after Rudolph's death to mind cutting a sorry figure in the public eye. Fortunately for him he had few acquaintances and spent much time in the woods alone; so at first he was scarcely aware of his unpopularity. But the neighbours were quick to point out to his parents what a dishonour their son had brought on the district; it had set the whole province by the ears, they said, and started a government enquiry as to why that part of the world had been so backward in sending volunteers to fight the Dragon. This touched to the quick many people who had never heard of Conrad, and who now realized they might be called on to display their heroism in front of the Castle, whether they would or no; for it was whispered that there might be an official round-up of likely young men.

His father and mother did their best to keep all this from Conrad. They were hurt and puzzled by his action, but they knew what a blow his brother's death had been, and did not want to distress him needlessly. But as he walked about the woods, especially at night time, he would hear a stone go whizzing by him, or see a stick break at his feet; and demanding the cause of these atten-tions from one of the culprits, a lad rather smaller than himself, he was told very fully and in words that hurt. His foolish letter had got the place a bad name and he himself was this, that, and the other.

Conrad tried to take no notice and go his own way, but at last he saw there was only one thing to do. He must challenge the Dragon himself.

He did not go into training, as his brothers had done, with walks before breakfast and nourishing, unappetizing food; he did not, if he chanced to spy a fantastic-looking bush, set spurs to his horse and with a wild cry aim at it with his axe. Had he made the experiment he would have fallen off, for his horsemanship had not improved. Nor did he spend his savings on the purchase of costly weapons, and military equipment of plume, breastplate, and golden epaulette, to charm the spectator's eye. His preparations were quite simple and only one of them cost him thought. This was the speech he would have to make at the foot of the steps.

He knew that it must be a declaration of love, or the Dragon would ignore it. But since Rudolph's death his indifference to the Princess had deepened into positive dislike, almost hatred. He could not bring himself to say he loved her, even without meaning it. So he set himself to devise a form of words which would sound to the greedy, stupid Dragon sufficiently like praise, but to him, the speaker, would mean something quite different.

A letter came written on parchment under a great red seal, calling him by flattering terms, and fixing three o'clock as the hour for the contest. Conrad started early, before the November morning was well astir. He was riding the horse his father had lent him; the Dragon did not care for horses. Conrad would have felt safer on foot, but besides his lunch he had an axe to carry, and the Castle was seventeen miles away. He was wearing his old suit, as it seemed a pity to spoil his best one. As he went along, mostly walking, but occasionally trotting, if the horse stumbled, people stopped work or came out of their houses to look at him. They knew why he was there, and though they did not cheer or clap, they did not insult or ridicule him, which was some comfort.

But when six hours later the portals of the ravine opened before him, the Castle burst into view, and the whole scene, branded so long on his memory, renewed itself, and at such dreadfully close quarters his heart sank. He had not been able to eat his lunch, and still carried it (having been taught not to throw food away) in a satchel hung round his neck. This embarrassed him, for he thought the onlookers would laugh. But at present there were very few onlookers; the spectacle had become so common, it hardly awakened any interest.

But when he was near enough to the flight of stairs to be able to distinguish the separate steps the crowd began to thicken somewhat. A little boy blew a sudden blast on a tin trumpet in the very ear of Conrad's horse. It pranced about in alarm, and Conrad, clutching wildly at its mane and neck, was ignominiously thrown. He was rather shaken, but not too much shaken to hear the crowd laugh and ask each other what sort of champion this was who couldn't sit on his horse properly.

Conrad dare not remount his horse, for fear of falling off; and a good-natured man offered to lead it for him a few paces in the rear, so that he could get on if he liked. He was glad to be rid of it on such easy terms. But he was aware of cutting an awkward figure on foot, in dusty clothes, trailing an axe which he tried to use as a walking stick. The crowd, who liked its champions gay, reckless and handsome, received him coldly. He felt they grudged their admiration and withheld their goodwill.

(But in the Castle the Princess Hermione, her face pressed against the window-pane, watched every inch of his progress. "It's he; it's Conrad. I knew it was!" she cried. "You must let me wait another moment, Magician. Just one more moment!")

Conrad was trying to distract his mind by repeating over and over the address he meant to deliver to the Princess. He had a copy of the speech in his cap, to read if his mind became a blank. He wished he could do something to please the spectators, besides smiling nervously at them, for he carried in his pocket a phial of chloroform, wrapped in a handkerchief; he meant to break and wave this in the Dragon's face before using the axe. None of his predecessors had attacked it with anything but cold steel. Suddenly he was aware that the horse was no longer following. The man had drawn it to one side and was standing in front of it, his hands over its eyes. The crowd had fallen back. Conrad had reached the steps. The Castle clock struck three.

He kneeled down, took off his cap, and said:

"Most Wonderful Princess, this is a moment I have long looked forward to, with what feelings you best may guess. The many who have kneeled here before me have been eloquent in your praise; who am I to add a syllable to their tributes? But I know it is not the words you value, most discerning Princess, but the heart that inspires them."

At this moment the rock heaved, the Dragon came forth and hung over Conrad with lolling tongue. He could feel its hot breath on his cheek. The words died on his lips, he stared wildly round, then remembered the cue in his cap, and went on without looking up:

"All have loved you well, but some (dare I say it) have voiced their love less happily than others. They said: 'This, my love, though great, is but an acorn that will grow with years into an oak.' But when I remember what you have done for me: rescued me from the dull round of woodland life; raised me from obscurity into fame; transformed me from a dreamer into a warrior, an idler into a hunter of Dragons; deigned to make yourself the limit of my hopes and the end of my endeavours, I have no words to thank you, and I cannot love you more than I do now!"

The more sensitive in the crowd had already turned away. The hardier spirits, with eyes glued to the scene, saw an unfamiliar thing. The Dragon swayed, dipped, hesitated. Its tongue licked the dust at Conrad's feet. He who had hitherto done nothing to defend himself drew out the handkerchief and threw it awkwardly but with lucky aim, right into the Dragon's scarlet mouth. The beast roared, snorted, coughed, whimpered, and in a moment looked less terrible. Conrad, taking heart, lifted the axe and struck at the scaly neck towering above him. It was a clumsy blow, unworthy of a woodman, but it found its mark. A torrent of green blood gushed out, evaporating before it reached the ground. The Dragon's claws lost their hold on the rock, and it sprawled outwards, exposing a long, black tubular body no one had seen till now. The neck dropped to within easy reach of Conrad's axe, and, encouraged by the frenzied cheering behind him, he hacked at it again and again. Its balance lost, the Dragon seemed bewildered and helpless; a child could have tackled it; it was as passive under the axe as a felled tree. Conrad seemed to be having matters all his own way, when suddenly the Dragon made a convulsive movement and wriggled backwards into the rock, which closed over it. Conrad was left in possession of the field.

The crowd stopped cheering; no one quite knew what to do; least of all Conrad, who was still standing by the steps, half-dazed. That the Dragon had retired wounded and discomfited was plain to all; but perhaps it was only biding its time, gathering its strength for a fresh attack. It had so long seemed invincible; they could not believe it was dead.

But when seconds passed and nothing happened they began to surge round Conrad, weeping and laughing and trying to take his hand. From the Castle, too, came signs of rejoicing; a faint cheering and fluttering of handkerchiefs, then a full-throated roar, and flags waved from every window. A little throng began to form at the top of the steps, the King in the centre, his sceptre in his hand and his crown on his head. They were all laughing and talking together; it was clear they had never expected Conrad to win. They had made no plans for his reception. They called and beckoned to him to come up; but he did not understand, so the crowd came behind and pushed him. As he moved up the King came down alone; they met in midstair; the King kissed Conrad and embraced him, and they walked up to the Castle arm-in-arm.

"And now I must present you to my daughter," the King was saying as they reached the top, and the members of the Court were pressing forward with shining eyes to congratulate the victor of the Dragon. "Where is she? She's away somewhere; she'll come in a minute. Silly child, she's missed all the fun."

"Hermione! Hermione!" called the ladies of the Court, in their light, eager voices, peering into the hall, staring up at the windows. And the crowd, nearly ninety feet below, took up the cry, "Hermione! We want Princess Hermione!" It was an immense crowd now, for all the town was running to the spot, and the volume of sound was terrific.

But still she delayed. The crowd shouted itself hoarse; the ladies of the Court coughed and wrinkled up their faces and looked appealingly at each other; the King frowned slightly, for he felt she ought to be here now; but still the Princess did not come.

Then they all burst out excitedly: "Where can she be?" "Let's go and look for her," while others said: "No, no; the shock would harm her; we must break it to her gradually."

There was quite a little confusion and uproar of voices arguing this way and that, stirring the general gaiety to an even higher pitch. They flocked into the Castle, dividing hither and thither, their silvery laughter lost among the corridors and colonnades.

Conrad had been torn from the King's side and hurried into the building before he knew what was doing. Several people promised to show him the way, but when they had gone a little distance they forgot about him, and flew off, with shouts of laughter, to join their own friends. Conrad seemed to be alone in the long dark corridor, but when he looked round there was a man standing at the far end of it. Conrad walked towards him, calling out to him to wait; but the fellow hurried on, though how he could go like that, his face looking backwards all the time, Conrad did not understand.

Through doors, along passages, down steps they went; always with the same distance between them, always getting lower and lower; Conrad felt the cold on his cheeks and hands. At last a door indistinguishable from the surrounding masonry opened, showing a room. Conrad followed his guide in, then lost sight of him.

On a couch by the wall lay the Princess, her head turned away, and in the whiteness of her neck a gash dreadful to behold. On the wall above her lay the shadow to which her indescribable beauty had lent a kind of life; it could not long survive her, and just as Conrad took in the perfection of its loveliness it faded from the wall.

He fell on his knees by the bed. How long he knelt he could not tell, but when he looked up the room was full of people.

"You have killed her," someone said.

Conrad rose and faced them.

"I did not kill her; I killed the Dragon."

"Look," said another voice: "She has the same wound in her neck."

"That wound I gave the Dragon."

"And what is this?" asked a third, pointing to a ball of linen, tightly grasped in Princess Hermione's outstretched hand. He took it and shook it out; the smell of chloroform filled the air. A cluster of eyes read the name in the corner of the handkerchief—Conrad's.

"And you poisoned her as well!" they gasped.

"That poison," said Conrad, "I gave to the Dragon."

One or two nodded their heads; but the rest shouted:

"But you *must* have killed her! How else did she die?"

Conrad passed his hand across his face.

"Why should I kill her? I love her," he said in a broken voice. "It was the Dragon I killed."

Then, as they all gazed at him fascinated, he added:

"But the Dragon was the Princess."

Immediately there was a terrible hubbub, and to shouts of "Liar", "Murderer", "Traitor", Conrad was hustled from the room.

★

A story was put about that the Princess had somehow met her death defending Conrad from the Dragon; and Conrad, when asked if this was so, would not altogether deny it. His hour of popularity as slayer of the Dragon soon passed, and in its place he incurred a lasting unpopularity of having been somehow concerned in the Princess's death. "He ought never to have used that chloroform," was a criticism repeated with growing indignation from mouth to mouth. It was a mark of patriotism to make light of the the Dragon's misdeeds, for their long continuance redounded little to the country's credit and capacity. They were speedily forgotten, while the fame of Princess Hermione, a national treasure, went mounting ever higher in the hearts of her countrymen.

The Hoard

J. R. R. TOLKIEN

Two of the best modern Dragons are Smaug who guards the treasure in "The Hobbit" and the dragon "who had a wicked heart" in "Farmer Giles of Ham". Both these books must be read in their entirety, to enjoy their dragons fully. But here is a story in verse about another dragon.

When the moon was new and the sun young
of silver and gold the gods sung:
in the green grass they silver spilled,
and the white waters they with gold filled.
Ere the pit was dug or Hell yawned,
ere dwarf was bred or dragon spawned.
there were Elves of old, and strong spells
under green hills in hollow dells
they sang as they wrought many fair things,
and the bright crowns of the Elf-kings.
But their doom fell, and their song waned,
by iron hewn and by steel chained.
Greed that sang not, nor with mouth smiled,
in dark holes their wealth piled,
graven silver and carven gold;
over Elvenhome the shadow rolled.

There was an old dwarf in a dark cave,
to silver and gold his fingers clave;

246

with hammer and tongs and anvil-stone
he worked his hands to the hard bone,
and coins he made, and strings of rings,
and thought to buy the power of kings.
But his eyes grew dim and his ears dull
and the skin yellow on his old skull;
through his bony claw with a pale sheen
the stony jewels slipped unseen.
No feet he heard, though the earth quaked,
when the young dragon his thirst slaked,
and the stream smoked at his dark door.
The flames hissed on the dank floor,
and he died alone in the red fire;
his bones were ashes in the hot mire.

There was an old dragon under grey stone;
his red eyes blinked as he lay alone.
His joy was dead and his youth spent,
he was knobbed and wrinkled, and his limbs bent
in the long years to his gold chained;
in his heart's furnace the fire waned.
To his belly's slime gems stuck thick,
silver and gold he would snuff and lick:
he knew the place of the least ring
beneath the shadow of his black wing.
Of thieves he thought on his hard bed,
and dreamed that on their flesh he fed,
their bones crushed, and their blood drank:
his ears drooped and his breath sank.
Mail-rings rang. He heard them not.
A voice echoed in his deep grot:
a young warrior with a bright sword
called him forth to defend his hoard.

His teeth were knives, and of horn his hide,
but iron tore him, and his flame died.

There was an old king on a high throne:
his white beard lay on knees of bone;
his mouth savoured neither meat nor drink,
nor his ears song; he could only think
of his huge chest with carven lid
where pale gems and gold lay hid
in secret treasury in the dark ground;
its strong doors were iron-bound.
The swords of his thanes were dull with rust,
his glory fallen, his rule unjust,
his halls hollow, and his bowers cold,
but king he was of elvish fold.
He heard not the horns in the mountain pass,
he smelt not the blood on the trodden grass,
but his halls were burned, his kingdom lost;
in a cold pit his bones were tossed.

There is an old hoard in a dark rock,
forgotten behind doors none can unlock;
that grim gate no man can pass.
On the mound grows the green grass;
there sheep feed and the larks soar,
and the wind blows from the sea-shore.
The old hoard the Night shall keep,
while earth waits and the Elves sleep.

The Dragon Speaks

C. S. LEWIS

The most unexpected and memorable of modern Dragons may be found in "The Voyage of the 'Dawn Treader'." Eustace's terrible adventure must be read as part of the book, and would be spoilt if cut out and stuck in here. But this collection of Dragons can have no better ending than the sad confession of an old, lonely dragon which C. S. Lewis wrote years before he had discovered the wonderful land of Narnia.

Once the worm-laid egg shattered in the wood.
I came forth shining into the trembling wood;
The sun was on my scales, dew upon the grasses,
The cold, sweet grasses and the sticky leaves.
I loved my speckled mate. We played at druery
And sucked warm milk dripping from the ewes' teats.

Now I keep watch on the gold in my rock cave
In a country of stones: old, deplorable dragon
Watching my hoard. In winter night the gold
Freezes through tough scales my cold belly;
Jagged crowns, cruelly twisted rings,
Icy and knobb'd, are the old dragon's bed.

Often I wish I had not eaten my wife
(Though worm grows not to dragon till he eats worm).
She could have helped me, watch and watch about,
Guarding the gold; the gold would have been safer.

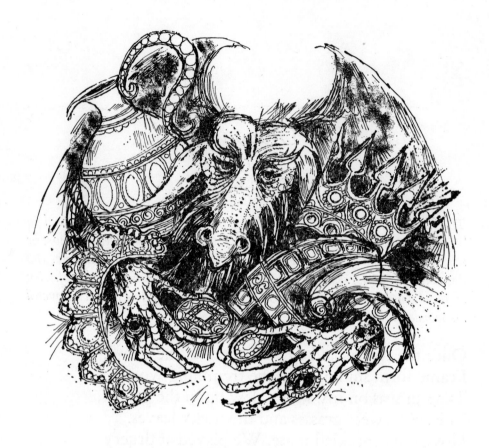

I could uncoil my tired body and take
Sometimes a little sleep when she was watching.

Last night under the moonset a fox barked,
Startled me; then I knew I had been sleeping.
Often an owl flying over the country of stones
Startles me; then I think that I must have slept,
Only a moment. That very moment a Man
Might have come from the towns to steal my gold.

They make plots in the towns to take my gold,
They whisper of me in the houses, making plans,

Merciless men. Have they not ale upon the benches,
Warm wives in bed, and song, and sleep the whole night?
I leave my cave once only in the winter
To drink at the rock pool; in summer twice.

They have no pity for the old, lugubrious dragon.
Lord that made the dragon, grant me thy peace,
But say not that I should give up the gold,
Nor move, nor die. Others would have the gold.
Kill me rather, Lord, the Men and the other dragons;
Then I can sleep; go when I will to drink.

Epilogue

AND I saw an angel come down from Heaven, having the key of the bottomless pit and a great chain in his hand. And he laid hold on the Dragon, that old serpent which is the Devil, and bound him a thousand years, and cast him into the bottomless pit, and shut him up, and set a seal upon him that he should deceive the nations no more, till the thousand years should be fulfilled. . . .

And when the thousand years are expired, the Dragon shall be loosed out of his prison, and shall go out to deceive the nations which are in the four quarters of the earth, Gog and Magog, to gather them together to battle: the number of whom is as the sand of the sea.

And they went up on the breadth of the earth, and compassed the camp of the Saints about, and the Beloved City: and fire came down from God out of Heaven, and devoured them.

And the Dragon that deceived them was cast into the lake of fire and brimstone, where the Beast and the False Prophet are, and shall be tormented day and night for ever and ever.

The Revelation of St. John.

Notes on Sources

Except where otherwise stated, I have myself adapted the stories in the first three parts of this book from the various sources indicated. I have tried to present them as accurately as possible, adding nothing but some dialogue on occasions when this was lacking and seemed necessary; omitting where stories were too long, and sometimes cutting incidents that did not have any bearing on the part of the story which concerned dragons.

Dedication: From "The Alliterative Metre" by C. S. Lewis. *Rehabilitations* (1939) page 122. First published in *Lysistrata* Vol. II, p. 16. May 1935.

Jason and the Dragon of Colchis: Adapted and combined from the *Argonautica* of Apollonius Rhodius, Book III, and that ascribed to Orpheus, with some help from Ovid's *Metamorphoses*, Book VII, and shorter references in Pindar, Apollodorus, Valerius Flaccus and Hyginus.

The Song of Orpheus: This is a rather free rendering of Orphic Hymn number LXXXV. Lang ascribes it, erroneously, to the Orphic Argonautica. It first appeared in his *The Story of the Golden Fleece* in the *St. Nicholas Magazine*, Feb: 1891, reprinted as a separate book in 1903, and included in *Tales of Troy and Greece*, 1907. The poem alone was included in the second edition of his *Grass of Parnassus*, 1892, and his *Poetical Works*, 1923, Vol. II, p. 213.

The Boy and the Dragon: Retold from Aelianus, *Of the Nature of Animals*, Book VI, Chapter 63. Aelian lived in Italy (though he wrote in Greek) in the 3rd Century A.D.

The Dragon of Macedon: Retold from Aelianus, Book X, Chapter 48.

The Fox and the Dragon: Phaedrus, *Fable* XXI. *The Dragon and the Peasant* and *The Dragon's Egg:* from later compilations of Classical Fables. See B. E. Perry: *Babrius and Phaedrus*, Loeb Classical Library, No. 436; 1965.

Dragons and Elephants: From Herodotus, Book III, Chapter 116; Pliny,

Natural History, Book VIII, Chapters 11–12 (translated by Philemon Holland, 1601); Lucan, *Pharsalia*, Book IX, lines 726–32; Propertius, *Elegy* VIII; Aelian II, 16, etc.; Philostratus, *Images*, Book II, Chapter 17.

Sigurd the Dragon-Slayer: Retold shortly from the *Volsunga Saga* and the *Prose Edda*.

Beowulf and the Dragon: Retold from the original Anglo-Saxon epic.

Ragnar Shaggy-Legs and the Dragons: Retold from Saxo Grammaticus, *The Danish History*, Book IX, Section 302, written about 1200 A.D.

An Adventure of Digenes the Borderer: Retold from John Mavrogordato's edition of the medieval Byzantine Greek epic of *Digenes Akrites*, Book VI, lines 41–85.

The Red Dragon of Wales: Combined and retold from *The Story of Lludd and Llevelys* in *The Mabinogion* (Lady Charlotte Guest's version) and Nennius, *History of the Britons*, sections 40–42, and Geoffrey of Monmouth's *British History*, Bk. VI, Chapters 17–19 and Book VII, Chapter 3. Nennius wrote in the 9th Century, and Geoffrey about 1150 A.D.

Sir Tristram in Ireland: Retold from Jessie L. Weston's translation of the old German romance of *Tristram and Iseult* by Godfried von Strassburg, composed about the year 1210 A.D., the translation first published 1899.

Sir Launcelot and the Dragon: From *Le Morte d'Arthur*—(*The Works of Sir Thomas Malory*, edited by Eugene Vinaver, 1947, Vol. II, pp. 791–4) Book XI, Chapters 1–2. Malory's work was completed in 1469 and published by Caxton in 1485. I have modernized the spelling.

St. George and the Dragon: Adapted from Alexander Barclay's verse *Life of St. George* (1515) and various ballads.

The Mummer's Play: The Oxfordshire St. George Play, taken down orally by F. G. Lee and first published in *Notes and Queries*, 5th Series, Vol. II, p. 503, 1874. I have used as prologue and epilogue Kenneth Grahame's account of the Mummers in "Snowbound", first published in *The National Observer* 23 Sept: 1893, and collected in his *Pagan Papers* (1893) and *The Golden Age* (1895).

Sir John Maundeville's Dragon: Chapter III and most of Chapter IV of *The Voiage and Travayle of Syr John Maundeville, Knight* (1568): probably written, in French, by Jean d'Outremeuse (1338–1400). I have modernized the spelling.

The Dragons of Rhodes, Lucerne and Somerset: Retold from *Mundus Subterraneus* Book VIII, Chapter 27, by Athanasius Kircher (1601–1680). "Victor and the Dragon of Lucerne" is adapted from Kircher's account in *Mundus*

Subterraneus; and "The Dragon of Shervage Wood" from the version quoted by K. M. Briggs in her *The Fairies in Tradition and Literature* (1967) p. 67.

The Laidly Worm, *The Lambton Worm* and *The Little Bull-Calf* are taken, unaltered, from *English Fairy Tales* (1890) and *More English Fairy Tales* (1894) (numbers XXXIII, LXXXV and LXXIV) collected and retold by Joseph Jacobs.

The Dragon and his Grandmother: is the translation from Grimms' *Household Tales*, No. CXXVII, made by May Sellar for Andrew Lang's *The Yellow Fairy Book* (1894).

The Dragon of the North: Retold from the version of "Der Norlands Drache" from Kreutzwald's *Esthnishe Mahrchen* given in *The Yellow Fairy Book* (1894).

The Master Thief and the Dragon: Retold from the J. G. von Hahn version in *Griechische und Albanesische Marchen* given in *The Pink Fairy Book* (1897).

Stan Bolovan and the Dragon: Retold from the version of the Rumanian folk tale in *The Violet Fairy Book* (1901).

The Prince and the Dragon: Retold from the version of the Serbian folk tale in *The Crimson Fairy Book* (1903).

The Cock and the Dragon: Retold from the version in Leslie Bonnet's *Chinese Fairy Tales* (1958).

The Chinese Dragons: Most of the quotations from ancient Chinese sources are from Chapter VII of Charles Gould's *Mythical Monsters* (1886). Lu Keui-meng's fable of the Dragon-Keeper is retold from the version in *The Dragon Book* compiled by E. D. Edwards (1938)—in spite of the book's title, this is the only dragon story in it.

The Red Cross Knight and the Dragon: *The Faerie Queene* (1590) by Edmund Spenser, Book I, Canto XI. Stanzas 8–14, and 52–55. The prose links are quoted from Mary MacLeod's *Stories from the Faerie Queene* (1897).

The Shepherd of the Giant Mountains: This long narrative poem by Menella Bute Smedley, based on a German original by De la Motte Fouqué, was published in *Sharpe's London Magazine* 7 March and 21 March 1846; Vol. I, pp. 298–300, 326–8.

Jabberwocky: From *Through the Looking-Glass and What Alice Found There* (1872) by Lewis Carroll; pp. 21–24.

The Lady Dragonissa: My Own Fairy Book (1895) by Andrew Lang, pp. x–xiii.

The Fiery Dragon: The Book of Dragons (1900) by E. Nesbit, pp. 223–56. First published in *The Strand Magazine*, Vol. XVIII, pp. 347–55, September 1899.

The Dragon at Hide and Seek: This story by G. K. Chesterton was first published in *Number Two Joy Street* (1924) pp. 38–49.

Conrad and the Dragon: This story by L. P. Hartley was first published in *The Children's Cargo*, edited by Lady Cynthia Asquith (1930), pp. 76–114.

The Hoard: The Adventures of Tom Bombadil, and Other Verses (1962) by J. R. R. Tolkien, pp. 53–6.

The Dragon Speaks: The Pilgrim's Regress (1933) by C. S. Lewis, pp. 248–9.

Epilogue: The Revelation of St. John the Divine. Chapter XX, Verses 1–3; 7–10.

Acknowledgements

The Editor and Publishers are indebted to the following for permission to include copyright material in this book:

Cambridge University Press for permission to include an extract from *Selected Literary Essays* by C. S. Lewis, originally published by the Oxford University Press in *Rehabilitations*; The Bodley Head Ltd. and Curtis Brown Ltd. for permission to include an extract from *The Golden Age* by Kenneth Grahame; John Farquharson Ltd. on behalf of the Estate of the late E. Nesbit for permission to include "The Fiery Dragon" by E. Nesbit from *The Book of Dragons*; Miss D. Collins and Basil Blackwell Ltd. for permission to include "The Dragon at Hide and Seek" by G. K. Chesterton from *Number Two Joy Street*; the Author and Hamish Hamilton Ltd. for permission to include "Conrad and the Dragon" by L. P. Hartley from *Collected Stories*; George Allen & Unwin Ltd., London and Houghton Mifflin Company, Boston, U.S.A. for permission to include "The Hoard" by J. R. R. Tolkien from *The Adventures of Tom Bombadil*; Geoffrey Bles Ltd., London and William R. Eerdmans Publishing Co., Michigan, U.S.A. for "The Dragon Speaks" by C. S. Lewis from *The Pilgrim's Regress*.